Homilies on the
First Epistle of John

THE WORKS OF SAINT AUGUSTINE
A Translation for the 21st Century

Part III — Homilies

Volume 14: Homilies on the First Epistle of John

The English translation of the works of Saint Augustine has been made possible with contributions from the following:

Order of Saint Augustine

Province of Saint Thomas of Villanova (East)

Province of Our Mother of Good Counsel (Midwest)

Province of Saint Augustine (California)

Province of Saint Joseph (Canada)

Vice Province of Our Mother of Good Counsel

Province of Our Mother of Good Counsel (Ireland)

Province of Saint John Stone (England and Scotland)

Province of Our Mother of Good Counsel (Australia)

The Augustinians of the Assumption (North America)

The Sisters of Saint Thomas of Villanova

Order of Augustinian Recollects

Province of Saint Augustine

Mr. and Mrs. James C. Crouse

Mr. and Mrs. Paul Henkels

Mr. and Mrs. Francis E. McGill, Jr.

Mr. and Mrs. Mariano J. Rotelle

THE WORKS OF SAINT AUGUSTINE

A Translation for the 21st Century

Homilies on the First Epistle of John

(Tractatus in Epistolam Joannis ad Parthos)

I/14

introduction, translation and notes by
Boniface Ramsey
(series editor)

editors
Daniel E. Doyle, O.S.A.
and Thomas Martin, O.S.A.

New City Press
Hyde Park, New York

Published in the United States by New City Press
202 Comforter Blvd., Hyde Park, New York 12538
©2008 Augustinian Heritage Institute

Cover design by Leandro De Leon
Cover picture: Ottaviano Nelli, *Saint Augustine preaches to the people*
(Gubbio, Italy, Saint Augustine Church)

Library of Congress Cataloging-in-Publication Data:
Augustine, Saint, Bishop of Hippo.
  The works of Saint Augustine.
  "Augustinian Heritage Institute"
  Includes bibliographical references and indexes.
  Contents: — pt. 3, v .15. Expositions of the Psalms, 1-32
—pt. 3, v. 1. Sermons on the Old Testament, 1-19.
— pt. 3, v. 2. Sermons on the Old Testament, 20-50 — [et al.] — pt. 3,
v. 10 Sermons on various subjects, 341-400.
    1.   Theology — Early church, ca. 30-600.   I. Hill,
Edmund. II. Rotelle, John E.   III. Augustinian
Heritage Institute.   IV. Title.
BR65.A5E53   1990   270.2   89-28878

ISBN 978-1-56548-055-1   (series)
ISBN   978-1-56548-283-3   (cloth)
ISBN 978-1-56548-289-0 (paperback)

3rd Printing December 2019

Printed in the United States of America

For my friends

Princess Alexandra Schönburg
and Taki Theodoracopulos

with affection and gratitude

Contents

Introduction

Among Augustine's most important homilies are the series of ten that he preached on the First Epistle of John during the course of Easter Week and for two days sometime after Easter Week (see IX,1). They were probably given in the evenings, when an audience would have had more leisure to listen to a longer sermon,[1] and scholars seem to have settled on 407 as the year in which they were delivered.[2] Inasmuch as Easter Week homilies often addressed those who had been baptized at the Easter Vigil and were intended to deepen their understanding of what had occurred at that moment, it makes sense to ask whether the *Homilies on the First Epistle of John* were intended to be mystagogical catecheses—i.e., explanations of the Easter sacraments, or mysteries (as they were often called), to those who had just participated in them. There is sufficient mention of new life, enlightenment, anointing, water and other baptismal themes, as well as of the parameters of the Christian community and the demands of Christian morality, in the epistle for one to speculate or deduce that Augustine intended this commentary primarily for mystagogical use.[3] And, while preaching on it, Augustine does in fact make a number of references to baptism, some more direct than others (I,5; II,9; III,1.5.12; IV,8.11-12; V,6-7; VI,10-11, VII,6.11), at least two of which (II,9; VI,10) can be construed as alluding to a recent event.

If these homilies are mystagogies, however, they are certainly not in the style of Ambrose or Cyril of Jerusalem, to name two of the most well-known examples, which is marked by a more or less systematic presenta-

---

1. See S. Poque, "Les lectures liturgiques de l'octave pascale à Hippone d'après les traités de S. Augustin sur la première épître de S. Jean" *Revue Bénédictine* 74 (1964) 222-226. The reference in I,12 to the fatigue that Augustine's listeners might be experiencing adds to the probability that these sermons were given toward the end of the day.
2. Until relatively recently the tendency was to attribute the sermons to sometime in the second decade of the fifth century.
3. The possibility that the epistle has a baptismal thrust is discussed in Raymond E. Brown, *The Epistles of John* = Anchor Bible 30 (New York: Doubleday, 1982) 43-45, 242-245. Brown is partially sympathetic to the views of W. Nauck, who, among other things, argues in favor of a baptismal aspect to the epistle in *Die Tradition und der Character des ersten Johannesbriefes* (Tübingen: Mohr, 1957).

tion of baptism. There are simply too few mentions of the sacrament, and none after the seventh homily. At no point is there an extended discussion of the baptismal liturgy, which was a central theme of the post-baptismal catecheses. Moreover, the homilies seem to presuppose listeners who are already experienced in the faith, whose most recent exposure to baptism was as onlookers rather than as recipients (see I,5; VI,10). It seems reasonable to conclude, then, that they are not mystagogical instructions. Neither are they like the many other sermons that Augustine preached during the course of Easter Week (224-260E, 375B),[4] which are not mystagogical but which are nonetheless either at least partially directed to the newly baptized, or emphasize baptism or aspects of the Easter liturgy such as the singing of the Alleluia, or focus on the resurrected Christ and his appearances. There are two references to the Alleluia in the present homilies (V,7; VIII,1), it is true, but only the second of them is specifically paschal. There is no mention of the resurrected Christ or of the events associated with the resurrection that points to an Easter context and that would not fit just as well in a standard Sunday or weekday sermon. The conclusion must be, then, that Augustine's *Homilies on the First Epistle of John* are merely sermons on a particular book of the New Testament that are by and large unrelated to the liturgical season in which they were preached.

In fact this is the earliest extended work, whether in the form of sermons or commentary, on this book of scripture that has survived to our day. It seems surprising that the prolific Origen, who produced a lengthy commentary on the Gospel of John early in the third century, wrote nothing on the epistle attributed to the same author. Diodore of Tarsus, who died in the 390s, was said to have commented on it, but, if that is the case, his writing disappeared without a trace. The famous Alexandrian exegete Didymus the Blind, who died a few years later than Diodore, apparently wrote a commentary on all three Johannine epistles, but there are no traces of it either.

As Augustine observes in his prologue, referring to the epistle's leitmotiv, John "said many things, and nearly everything was about charity." This was a theme that Augustine developed with frequency,

---

4. These sermons are assigned to various years; some of them may not have been preached during Easter Week itself but rather during the Easter season.

and, in what seems to be his haste to get to it, by the end of his first homily he has already commented on about a fifth of the epistle, up to and beyond the place where John makes his first mention of love (2:5). It was also a theme that dovetailed with his Donatist preoccupations: Augustine saw the Donatist schism as, perhaps above all, a breach of charity.

A brief explanation of Donatism is owed here. At the very beginning of the fourth century, the Emperor Diocletian embarked upon a fierce persecution of his Christian subjects. One of the aspects of the persecution was the demand that copies of the Christian scriptures be handed over to the imperial authorities. Persons who gave up the scriptures in this way were labeled *traditores*—traitors or betrayers or "handers-over." Caecilian, the archdeacon of the Church in Carthage, where the persecution was particularly harsh, was accused of being a betrayer, as well as of having prevented food from being brought to Christians who were imprisoned for their faith. In 311 or 312 this same Caecilian was elected bishop of Carthage. Beyond his reputation, well-founded or not, there were a number of serious concerns regarding Caecilian's episcopal ordination, perhaps the most significant of which was that one of the bishops who ordained him, Felix of Aptunga, was himself accused of being a betrayer. Augustine makes very general references to these events in his homilies (I,12; X,10). In 312, a council of bishops in neighboring Numidia declared Caecilian deposed, although he ignored them and did not step down, and elected a certain Maiorinus in his place. Maiorinus died soon after, and Donatus was then elected to replace him. Meanwhile the new emperor, Constantine, who was sympathetic to the Christian religion, was supportive of Caecilian, and in 316 he made a formal judgment in his favor. Subsequently Constantine imposed sanctions on the Donatists, as they were beginning to be called on account of Donatus, the usurping bishop of Carthage, who was a strong and clever leader. In 321, however, Constantine resigned himself to the existence of the Donatists, since they were increasing in numbers and, practically speaking, could no longer be repressed, and he instituted a policy of toleration in their regard.

At this point a schism had been in effect for about a decade. But now, thanks in part to the new policy of toleration, which allowed the Donatists to flourish unhindered, there were two bishops—one for the

Catholics and another for the Donatists—not only in Carthage but also in many other places throughout North Africa. During the course of the fourth century the Donatists themselves experienced division within their own ranks, but their bishops nonetheless numbered in the hundreds. When Augustine first confronted them theologically, toward the end of the fourth century, they were at the onset of a gradual decline in influence. A council held in Carthage in 411, in which Augustine played a key role and which was attended by more than 500 bishops, both Catholic and Donatist, accelerated the decline. There may have been some revivals after that, but Donatism appears for all intents and purposes to have died out with the Arab invasions of North Africa in the seventh century.

As its history makes clear, Donatism was a fractious movement that could not conceive of a Church whose members, and especially whose hierarchy, were tainted by sinfulness. The Donatists embraced a lofty ideal of moral purity and claimed holiness as something unique to themselves (see I,8). In their eyes the Catholic Church lost its legitimacy by the alleged betrayal of Caecilian: neither its hierarchy nor its sacraments were valid any longer (see II,3). True to the universality that its name implied, however, Catholicism had the important advantage of being spread throughout the Mediterranean basin and beyond, whereas Donatism was a distinctly North African phenomenon, a point that Augustine makes repeatedly in these homilies (I,8.12-13; II,2-3; III,7; X,8.10) and elsewhere.

Augustine's selection of the First Epistle of John as the text for a series of sermons provided an ideal occasion for him to expose the fundamental lovelessness of Donatism by emphasizing that love fostered rather than destroyed unity, and that it brought with itself a tolerance of imperfection. Indeed, Augustine's choice of John—who spoke not only of love but also of division within the Church, division sufficiently serious to have prompted the very writing of the epistle[5]—may have been primarily motivated by the chance that it gave him to address the issue of

---

5. See Brown 47-115.

Donatism. Its presence throughout the homilies, whether direct or indirect, certainly suggests this.[6]

In discussing the love that is characteristic of the true Christian, Augustine makes use of three words or pairs of words: *amor/amare, dilectio/diligere* and *caritas*. In the present translation *amor* and *dilectio* have each been rendered as "love," and *amare* and *diligere* as "to love." *Caritas* has been translated as "charity." There is a fourth word as well, an intensive form of *amare*, which appears only once, in VIII,10, in the unusual context of the description of a woodworker who looks at a log and sees in it something that he wants to make; the woodworker, Augustine says, has fallen in love with (*adamavit*) the log.

In VIII,5 Augustine notes that *amor* tends to be used of fleshly love and hence does not designate real love at all, whereas *dilectio* is generally used for "better things." But he then immediately proceeds to show that the less noble associations of *amor* are often ignored when the word is employed. Earlier in the homilies, in fact, Augustine had spoken of *amor Dei* and *amor mundi*—the love of God and the love of the world – in tandem (II,8), and had done the same a few pages later with *dilectio Dei* and *dilectio mundi* (II,14). In another place he attributes *caritas*, normally a term of the loftiest qualifications, to irrational animals, although of course, as he observes, "it isn't spiritual but rather fleshly and innate" (IX,1). The Latin text of 1 Jn 4:8.16 ("God is love") reads *Deus dilectio est* in Augustine's version of the epistle. Soon after quoting 4:8 for the first time in VII,4, he rearranges the words in VII,6 to read *dilectio Deus est*, as he also does in IX,10 ("love is God," as the phrase is translated in both instances, seems to be demanded by the respective contexts, although from the perspective of regular Latin usage it could certainly be translated as "God is love"). In IX,1 he says, quoting either 4:8 or 4:16, that *Deus caritas est* ("God is charity"), after which he immediately reverts—as though the two ways of putting it were identical—to *Deus dilectio est*, and then again, in IX,2, he repeats *Deus caritas est*. For those who would demand complete verbal consistency, at the very least when

---

6. Augustine at least once, in II,5, when he addresses the issue of the eternal origin of the Son, also seems to have the Arians in mind, but he does not mention them by name there or anywhere else, except in VI,12, where he includes them in a brief list of heresies.

dealing with this most essential of concepts, Augustine's language here can be frustrating.[7]

With this vocabulary at his disposal, and using John's epistle as his point of departure, Augustine sets out to discuss love in its various manifestations. He expatiates upon the love that binds believers to the institution of the Church, upon the brotherly love that believers have for one another, upon love for enemies (which, he notes in VIII,4, is not directly mentioned in the epistle, although it is an important gospel theme; he resolves the discrepancy somewhat awkwardly in VIII,10), upon the love of human beings for God and of God for human beings, upon love for Christ, upon love for the world and its pleasures, and upon the love that animals display to one another. He also speaks of the relationship between love on the one hand and unity, pride, fear and faith on the other. He does not, however, discuss the love that the persons of the Trinity have for each other, nor the love of self, nor the love of friendship (although he makes passing references to friendship in VIII,5; IX,9; X,7). For an analysis of these forms of love we must look elsewhere in Augustine's writings. The present work, then, is not comprehensive in its treatment of its most important topic, nor, undoubtedly, was it ever intended to be such.

The phrase from these homilies that has resounded through the centuries is *dilige, et quod vis fac* ("love, and do what you want") (VII,8). Viewed within its context it is a perfectly acceptable and, indeed, appropriate statement. But it seems to have been intended to take its hearers aback, and the context itself, in which Augustine compares the first two persons of the Trinity with Judas and the disciplinary love of a father with the flattering attentiveness of a slave dealer (VII,7-8), likewise appears to have been calculated to administer a shock to those who were

---

7. See *The City of God* XIV,14, where Augustine states that scripture makes no distinction at all among *amor*, *dilectio* and *caritas*. He points out that in scripture both *amor* and *dilectio* can be used with either a positive or a negative thrust, yet he does not offer an example of *caritas* with a negative connotation. (Of course Augustine is referring to the Latin translation that he knew rather than to the Hebrew and Greek in which the Old and New Testaments were written.) But see also Sermon 349,1-2, in which, with no specific reference to scriptural usage, Augustine categorizes charity as both human and divine, the human in turn being divided into both lawful and unlawful.

listening to his words. It was often Augustine's method to emphasize a point by illustrating it with extreme examples (see, e.g., the absolute prohibition against lying in *Lying* 10-24; the fundamental indifference of physical misfortune and death in *The City of God* I,10-29), and that is certainly the case here.

The reader of the *Homilies on the First Epistle of John* will soon become aware of characteristics of the sermons that are common to ancient Christian commentaries on scripture. Thus Augustine allows the scriptural author to set the tone, as it were, by following him verse by verse, although he does not hesitate to devote much more time to some verses than to others and even to digress lengthily at various points. Throughout the homilies he uses other passages of scripture to illuminate the particular passage that he is examining at the moment, taking his illustrations freely from both the Old and New Testaments. On occasion he assumes that a given word has the same significance each time it appears in scripture, as when he discusses the term "end" in X,5 and seizes upon disparate examples of the word's usage from both the Psalms and Pauline literature. At other times he exhibits a certain flexibility in this regard, as when in VI,11 he notes that the term "water," which is of course frequent in scripture, has a variety of meanings depending on the context. Like many other Christian Latin speakers of his era, Augustine often appears to treat the Latin translation of the scriptures that he has before him as if it were no different than the original Hebrew or Greek; hence, in VIII,5 he gives the strong impression that, in Jn 21:15-17, when Jesus asked Peter whether he loved him, he asked the question in Latin![8]

But the *Homilies on the First Epistle of John* are not, in the end, a formal commentary on the text but rather an exercise in preaching (even though they were destined to be recorded in writing). As such, they are marvelous examples of the easy interaction that Augustine enjoyed with his congregation; they demonstrate his ability to adapt to the moment, to show how scripture spoke to contemporary issues, to present often-difficult material that he had mastered to his listeners in a

8. As *Teaching Christianity* II,11,16-13,20 shows, Augustine was well aware that translations should be accurate reflections of their originals, yet he also believed that divergent translations of a given passage could each express a truth.

way that they could understand, and to temper the exegetical with the spiritual.

These ten homilies could easily have been eleven or twelve. Augustine surely intended to provide a complete exposition of the epistle, but the manuscripts go only as far as his treatment of 5:2[9] (*Because we love God, and we carry out his commandments*), which he begins to discuss in X,4. In fact, although the tenth homily is of about average length, it ends abruptly in what appears to be the midst of an accusatory passage directed against the Donatists. It is safe to say, then, that this final homily is itself incomplete. Whether the abrupt ending of the manuscripts reflects an abrupt termination of Augustine's own preaching is unknown. Since he did not include his sermons as such in his *Revisions*, he does not comment there on his *Homilies on the First Epistle of John* and consequently says nothing about how they ended. At the conclusion of his translation Browne quotes six extended passages from other writings of Augustine that show how he treated some of the remaining verses of the epistle on different occasions; but the passages that Browne cites do not exhaust his views on the verses in question and hence could be misleading.[10]

The full Latin title by which Augustine's sermons are often designated is *Tractatus in Epistolam Joannis ad Parthos*—i.e., the *Tractates on John's Epistle to the Parthians*. Whereas tractates are drawn-out discussions of a particular topic, to which these homilies obviously conform, it is unclear why John's epistle is said to have been addressed to the Parthians, a little-known people who created an empire that occupied all of present-day Iran and much of its surrounding area at the time when the epistle was written. Yet Augustine himself refers elsewhere and without comment to the epistle in this way,[11] and Possidius, his friend of

---

9. The fifth chapter of the epistle has 21 verses.
10. E.g., Browne's citation from *Answer to Maximinus the Arian* II,22,3 might give the impression that Augustine interpreted *the Spirit, the water and the blood* of 5:8 solely in a Trinitarian way, whereas in Sermon 5,3 he views the same verse (which Browne does not cite) from a baptismal and ecclesiological perspective.
11. *Commentary on the Epistle to the Galatians* 40 ("Hence John says to the Parthians ... "); *Questions on the Gospels* II,39 ("That was also said by John in the Epistle to the Parthians ... ").

many years, includes *ad Parthos* in the title of the homilies in the *Indiculus*, his catalogue of Augustine's works.[12]

* * * * * * * * * * * * *

The Latin text for the present translation is found in *Sant'Agostino, Commento al Vangelo e alla Prima Epistola di San Giovanni* = Nuova Biblioteca Agostiniana, Opere di Sant'Agostino 24 (Rome: Città Nuova Editrice, 1968) 1627-1855, which is taken from the centuries-old Maurist edition, revised by Laura Muscolino. Among the most notable translations of these homilies into modern languages are those, in English, by H. Browne, revised by Joseph H. Myers, in A Select Library of the Nicene and Post-Nicene Fathers of the Christian Church 7 (reprinted Grand Rapids: Eerdmans, 1983) 453-529; John Burnaby, in *Augustine: Later Works* = Library of Christian Classics 6 (Philadelphia: Westminster Press, 1955) 251-348 (incomplete but extensive); and John W. Rettig, in *St. Augustine, Tractates on the Gospel of John 112-24; Tractates on the First Epistle of John* = Fathers of the Church 92 (Washington: Catholic University of America Press, 1995) 95-277; in French, by P. Agaësse, *Saint Augustin, Commentaire de la première épitre de s. Jean* = Sources Chrétiennes 75 (Paris: Editions du Cerf, 1961); in Spanish, by B. Martin Perez, *Exposición de la Epistola a los Partos* = Biblioteca de Autores Cristianos 187 (Madrid 1959); in Italian, by Giulio Madurini, in the Nuova Biblioteca Agostiniana volume cited above.

It should be mentioned that the translations of Augustine's biblical citations follow the Latin text that he had before him, which occasionally differs from the text in the original biblical languages. When he cites a verse differently at different moments, the English reflects this. Significant variations are footnoted.

---

12. See the discussion of the possible meanings of *ad Parthos* in Rettig 101-102.

Prologue

Your Holiness[1] recalls that we are accustomed to preach on the gospel according to John while observing the order of the text. But now the solemnity of the holy days[2] has intervened, when every year in the Church certain passages from the gospel have to be read, which means that others cannot be. The sequential order that we had embarked on, then, has had to be set aside for a short while but not abandoned.

When we were considering how to present the scriptures to you throughout this week, in keeping with the joyfulness of these days and as much as the Lord deigns to bestow, the epistle of Blessed John occurred to me, because it could be completed during these seven or eight days. Thus, while briefly setting aside his gospel, we shall not depart from him as we preach on his epistle[3]—especially because in that epistle there is enough that is flavorful for all those whose heart's palate, where God's bread is tasted, is sound, and there is enough that is of note for God's holy Church; in particular, charity is commended. He said many things, and nearly everything was about charity.

The one who has it in himself to listen must certainly rejoice at what he hears. For this reading will be like oil on a flame: if there is anything that may be nursed in him, it is nursed, and grows, and lasts. Similarly, there are those for whom it must be like a flame to kindling: if once it didn't catch fire, now, having been touched by these words, it catches fire. For in some what is there is being nursed, while in others a fire breaks out if one is lacking, so that we may all rejoice in one charity.

---

1. "Your Holiness" (*sanctitas vestra*): this way of referring to one's listeners was common to the preachers of Christian antiquity, much as today it is customary to hear "Dearly beloved," "Brothers and sisters," "My dear friends in Christ." The term recurs in IX,1. See also "Your Charity" (*caritas vestra*) in I,3; III,7; IV,5.12; V,6.8; VI,6; VIII,10.11; IX,1.5.
2. The reference is to Easter week.
3. Christian antiquity usually took for granted that the author of the Gospel of John, whom (as, e.g., Augustine does in I,8 below) it identified with the "beloved disciple" of Jn 13:23 and elsewhere, was also the author of the three epistles bearing the name of John. Modern scholarship tends to be more skeptical on this matter.

Where there is charity there is peace, and where there is humility there is charity.

Now let us listen to [John], and let us address his words as the Lord prompts, so that you too may have a good understanding of them for yourselves.

First Homily

1. *What was from the beginning, what we have heard, and what we have seen with our eyes, and what our hands have touched of the Word of life* (1:1). Who touches the Word with his hands apart from the fact that *the Word was made flesh and dwelled among us* (Jn 1:14)? But this Word which was made flesh, so that it might be touched by our hands, began to be flesh from the Virgin Mary, yet it didn't begin to be the Word then, because [John] said, *What was from the beginning*. See if his epistle isn't confirmed by his gospel, where you just recently heard: *In the beginning was the Word, and the Word was with God* (Jn 1:1). Perhaps someone will understand this about *the Word of life* as though it were a way of speaking about Christ, not as though it was the very body of Christ that was touched by our hands. See what follows: *And life itself was manifested* (1:2). Christ, then, is the Word of life. And how was life manifested (for it was *from the beginning*)? Yet it wasn't manifested to human beings, but it was manifested to angels, who saw it and who fed on it as their bread. But what does scripture say?

Man has eaten the bread of angels (Ps 78:25). Life itself was manifested in flesh so that, by being manifested, the thing which can be seen by the heart alone may also be seen by the eyes, so that it may heal hearts. For the Word is seen by the heart alone, but flesh is also seen by bodily eyes. We were able to see flesh, but we were unable to see the Word. The Word was made flesh, which we would be able to see, so that what was in us— whereby we might see the Word—would be healed.

2. *And we have seen, and we are witnesses* (1:2). Perhaps some of the brothers who don't know Greek are unaware what the word for "witnesses" is in Greek. It is a religious term that is used by everyone, for those whom we call witnesses in Latin[1] are called martyrs in Greek. Now, who hasn't heard of martyrs, or in what Christian mouth does the word "martyrs" not daily dwell?[2] (And would that it might also dwell in our hearts such that we may imitate the martyrs' sufferings and not trample

---

1. The Latin for "witnesses" is *testes*.
2. The cult of the martyrs was strong throughout the ancient Church, but it was especially so in North Africa, and Augustine's words perhaps reflect that reality.

them underfoot![3]) This is why [John] said, *We have seen, and we are witnesses*: we have seen, and we are martyrs. For, by bearing witness on the basis of what they saw, and by bearing witness on the basis of what they heard from those who saw, the martyrs suffered everything that they suffered, since the witness itself was displeasing to the persons against whom it was borne. The martyrs are God's witnesses. God willed to have human beings as witnesses so that human beings might also have God as their witness.

We have seen, he says, *and we are witnesses*. Where did they see? In a manifestation. What does that mean, "in a manifestation"? In the sun —that is, in this light. But how could he who made the sun be seen in the sun if not for the fact that *he pitched his tent in the sun and, like a bridegroom coming forth from his marriage bed, rejoiced like a giant to run his course* (Ps 19:4-5)? He who made the sun was before the sun, he was before the morning star,[4] before all the stars, before all the angels. He is the true creator, because *everything was made through him, and apart from him nothing was made* (Jn 1:3). Thus he would be seen by the fleshly eyes that see the sun. He pitched his tent itself in the sun—that is, he showed his flesh in the manifestation of this light. And the marriage bed of that bridegroom was the Virgin's womb, because in that virginal womb two things were joined, a bridegroom and a bride, the bridegroom being the Word and the bride being flesh. For it is written, *And they shall be two in one flesh* (Gn 2:24), and the Lord says in the gospel, *Therefore they are no longer two but one flesh* (Mt 19:6). Isaiah also notes very well that these two are themselves one, for he speaks in the person of Christ and says, *He set a wreath upon me like a bridegroom, and like a bride he adorned me with an ornament* (Is 61:10). One person appears to be speaking, and he has made himself a bridegroom and has made himself a bride, because they aren't two but one flesh, for *the Word was made flesh and dwelled among us*. The Church is joined to that flesh, and Christ becomes the whole, head and body.

---

3. "Not trample them underfoot" (*non eos calcibus persequamur*): the Latin is not easy to understand and has been translated in several different ways. Rettig proposes a different translation but notes the variants.

4. See Ps 110:3.

3. *And we are witnesses,* [John] says, *and we announce to you the eternal life that was with the Father and was manifested in us* (1:2-3) —that is, manifested among us, which is more clearly expressed as "manifested to us." *What we have seen and heard, then, we announce to you* (1:3). Let Your Charity[5] pay heed: *What we have seen and heard, then, we announce to you.* They saw the Lord himself present in the flesh, and they heard words from the Lord's mouth, and they announced them to us. We also have heard, then, but we haven't seen. Are we therefore less fortunate than those who saw and heard? And why does [John] add: *So that you also may have fellowship with us* (1:3)? They saw, we didn't see, and yet we are in fellowship because we maintain a common faith. There was in fact one who, when he saw, didn't believe and wished to touch and thus to believe, and he said, *I won't believe unless I put my fingers in the place of the nails and touch his wounds* (Jn 20:25). And for a moment he who offers himself to be seen always by the eyes of angels offered himself to be touched for a moment by the hands of human beings. And that disciple touched him and cried out, *My Lord and my God!* (Jn 20:28) Because he touched the man, he confessed God. And the Lord—consoling us who are unable to touch him with our hand as he is now seated in heaven, although we can touch him by faith—said to him, *Because you have seen, you have believed. Blessed are those who do not see and who believe.* (Jn 20:29) It is we who were described, we who were designated. May there be in us, then, the blessedness that the Lord foretold would come to be. Let us hold firmly onto what we don't see, because those who have seen it are announcing it. *So that you also,* [John] says, *may have fellowship with us.* And what is there that is so great in having fellowship with human beings? Don't disdain it; see what he adds: *And so that our fellowship may be with God the Father and Jesus Christ his Son. And we are writing these things to you,* he says, *so that your joy may be full.* (1:3-4) He speaks of full joy in that very fellowship, in that very charity, in that very unity.

4. *And this is the message that we heard from him and announce to you* (1:5). What does this mean? They themselves saw, they touched the Word of life with their hands. He was from the beginning, and for a time the only

---

5. "Your Charity" (*caritas vestra*): see Prologue, note 1.

Son of God was made visible and tangible. For what purpose did he come, or what new thing did he declare to us? What did he want to teach? Why did he do what he did, so that the Word would be made flesh, so that God would suffer immeasurable indignities from human beings, so that he would endure their slaps from hands which he himself formed? What did he want to teach? What did he want to show? What did he want to proclaim? Let us listen, for, without the fruit of the precept, it is a diversion and not a strengthening of the mind[6] to listen to what Christ accomplished, that he was born for us and that he suffered for us. What great thing are you listening to? See with what fruit you are listening. What did he want to teach? What, to proclaim? Listen: *That God is light, and there is no darkness in him* (1:5). Now who would dare to say that there is darkness in God? Or what is light itself? Is he perhaps speaking of the sorts of things that pertain to these eyes of ours? *God is light,* says someone or other, and the sun is light, and the moon is light, and a lamp is light. It must be something much greater than these, much more excellent, and much more supereminent. As far as God is from creation, as far as its maker is from the thing made, as far as wisdom is from what was made by wisdom, so much farther beyond all else must be that light. And perhaps we shall be like it if we know what that light is, and if we devote ourselves to it, so that we may be enlightened by it, because by ourselves we are darkness,[7] and if we have been enlightened by it we can be light and not be confounded by it, since we are confounded in ourselves. Who is it that is confounded in himself? He who knows that he is a sinner. Who isn't confounded by it? He who is enlightened by it. What does it mean to be enlightened by it? He who now sees himself darkened by sins and longs to be enlightened by it approaches it, which is why the psalm says, *Approach him and be enlightened, and your faces will not blush* (Ps 34:5). But you won't blush at it if, when he shows you your shamefulness, your shamefulness displeases you, so that you seize upon his beauty. This is what he wants to teach.

5. Are we saying this too hastily? Let [John] show us in what follows. Recall from the beginning of our sermon that this epistle commends

---

6. "It is a diversion and not a strengthening of the mind": *avocamentum mentis est, non firmamentum.* This is the first of several word-plays in the homilies.
7. See Eph 5:8.

charity: *God is light,* it says, *and there is no darkness in him.* And what
had it said before that? *So that you may have fellowship with us, and so
that our fellowship may be with God the Father and Jesus Christ his Son.*
Furthermore, if God is light, and if there is no darkness in him, and if we
should have fellowship with him, and if darkness should be driven from
us, so that there may be light in us, since darkness cannot have fellowship
with light, then see what follows: *If we say that we have fellowship with
him, and we are walking in darkness, we are lying* (1:6). You also have
the apostle Paul saying: *What fellowship is there between light and darkness?* (2 Cor 6:14) You say that you have fellowship with God, and you
are walking in darkness, but *God is light, and there is no darkness in him.*
How, then, is there fellowship between light and darkness?

A person may say to himself, then, "What shall I do? How shall I be
light? I live in sins and in wickedness." A certain hopelessness and sadness
steals up on him, as it were. There is no salvation apart from fellowship
with God. *God is light, and there is no darkness in him.* Sins, though, are
darkness. As the Apostle says, the devil and his angels are princes of this
darkness.[8] He wouldn't call them princes of darkness unless they were
princes of sinners and lords of the wicked. What is there to do, then, my
brothers? There must be fellowship with God; there is no other hope for
eternal life. *God is light, and there is no darkness in him.* Wickedness,
however, is darkness. We are weighed down with wickedness, with the
result that we can have no fellowship with God. What hope is there, then?
Hadn't I promised that I would say something that would bring joy during
these days? If I don't say it, that is sadness. *God is light, and there is no
darkness in him.* Sins are darkness. What will become of us?

Let us listen in case [John] should offer some comfort, should lift us up,
should give us hope, lest we grow weak on our journey. For we are
hastening, and it is to our homeland that we are hastening, and, if we lose
hope of arriving there, we grow weak on account of that very hopelessness.
But he who wants us to arrive there, so that he may hold us safe in our
homeland, feeds us on the way. Let us listen, then: *If we say that we have
fellowship with him, and we are walking in darkness, we are lying, and we*

---

8. See Eph 6:12.

are not acting truthfully (1:6). We shouldn't say that we have fellowship with him if we are walking in darkness. *If we are walking in the light, just as he himself is in the light, we have fellowship with one another* (1:7). Let us walk in the light, just as he himself is in the light, so that we may be able to have fellowship with him. And what do we do with our sins? Listen to what follows: *And the blood of Jesus Christ his Son will cleanse us of every offense* (1:7). God has given us great security. Deservedly do we celebrate the Pasch, when the blood of the Lord was poured out by which we are cleansed of every offense. Let us be secure: the devil used to hold a bond of slavery against us, but it was erased by the blood of Christ. *The blood of his Son,* [John] says, *will cleanse us of every offense.* What does *of every offense* mean? Pay heed: see, in Christ's name all the sins of those who are called infants have already been cleansed through his blood, which they have now confessed.[9] They went in old, they came out new. What does it mean that they went in old and came out new? They went in as old people and they came out as infants. It was a worn-out old age, a hoary life, but an infancy of regeneration, a new life. But what is there for us to do? Past sins have been forgiven—not only theirs but ours as well. And, after the forgiveness and abolishment of all our sins, some have perhaps been contracted by living in this world in the midst of trials. Let a person do what he can, therefore. Let him confess what he is, so that he may be healed by him who always is what he is, for he always was, and [now] is, while we [once] were not, and [now] are.

6. For see what [John] says: *If we say that we do not have sin, we are deceiving ourselves, and the truth is not in us* (1:8). If you confess that you are a sinner, then, the truth is in you, for the truth itself is light. Your life hasn't yet shone forth in perfection, because there are sins in you, but nonetheless you have already begun to be enlightened, because the confession of your sins is in you. For see what follows: *If we confess our offenses, he is faithful and righteous, so that he may forgive us our offenses and cleanse us of all our wickedness* (1:8-9)—not only past sins but also if we have perhaps contracted any from this life, because, so long as a person bears

---

9. These and the next few lines refer to the events of baptism, and specifically to entering the baptismal pool and emerging from it. "Infants" (*infantes*) is a technical term for the newly baptized.

flesh, he cannot but have at least slight sins. But don't belittle what we are referring to as these slight sins. If you belittle them when you weigh them, shudder when you count them out. For many slight ones make a great one; many drops fill a river; many grains make a mass.[10] And what hope is there? Confession above all, lest anyone should consider himself righteous and, before the eyes of God who sees what is, a person who [once] was not and [now] is should lift his neck. Confession above all, therefore, and then love, because what has been said of charity? *Charity covers a multitude of sins* (1 Pt 4:8).

Let us see now whether [John] commends charity on account of the offenses that creep up on us, because charity alone extinguishes offenses. Pride extinguishes charity; consequently humility strengthens charity; charity extinguishes offenses. Humility pertains to confession, whereby we confess that we are sinners. It isn't humility to say this with our tongue, as though, were we to call ourselves righteous, we would displease people by reason of arrogance. This is what wicked persons and fools do: "I know for sure that I am righteous, but what shall I say in people's presence? If I say that I am righteous, who would bear it, who would put up with it? My righteousness is known to God, yet I ought to call myself a sinner not because I am but so that I may not be found hateful by reason of arrogance." Tell people what you are, tell God what you are, because, if you don't tell God what you are, God will condemn what he finds in you. Do you want him to condemn you? You yourself condemn. Do you want him to acknowledge you? You yourself acknowledge, so that you can say to God: *Turn your face away from my sins* (Ps 51:9). Tell him as well those words in the same psalm: *Because I acknowledge my wickedness* (Ps 51:3).

If we confess our offenses, he is faithful and righteous, who forgives us our offenses and cleanses us of all wickedness. If we say that we have not sinned, we make him a liar, and his word is not in us. (1:9-10) If you say, "I have not sinned," you make him a liar, while wanting to make yourself truthful. How can it happen that God is a liar and man is truthful when

---

10. See also *Homilies on the Gospel of John* XII,14; Letter 265,8. In *Summa Theologiae* I-II, q.88, a.4, Thomas Aquinas, while referring to Augustine and denying that he would have meant such a thing, comments that no amount of venial sins can constitute a mortal sin.

scripture contradicts this? *Every man is a liar; God alone is truthful* (Rom 3:4). God, then, is truthful of himself; you are truthful through God, for of yourself you are a liar.

7. And in case [John] seems to have given impunity to sins because he said, *He is faithful and righteous, who purifies us from all wickedness* (1:9), and people say to themselves, "Let's sin, let's do in security what we want to do, let Christ cleanse us: he is faithful and righteous; let him cleanse us from all wickedness," he takes your evil security away from you and introduces a beneficial fear. It is evil of you to wish to be secure; be anxious. For he is faithful and righteous in order to forgive us our offenses, if ever you should displease yourself and be changed until you are perfected. What follows, then? *My little children, I am writing these things to you so that you may not sin* (2:1). But perhaps sin creeps up on us from human life. What will happen then? What? Is there now to be hopelessness? Listen: *And if anyone sins*, he says, *we have an advocate with the Father, Jesus Christ the righteous, and he is the propitiator for our sins* (2:1-2).[11] He is our advocate, therefore. Be careful not to sin. If sin creeps up on you due to life's frailty, be vigilant at once, let it displease you at once, condemn it at once, and, when you have condemned it, you will come securely to the judge. There you have your advocate. Don't fear that you may lose your case once you have confessed. For, if there are times in this life when a person entrusts himself to a clever tongue and doesn't perish, will you entrust yourself to the Word and perish? Cry out: *We have an advocate with the Father!*

8. See how John himself observes humility. He was, to be sure, a righteous and great man, who drank in hidden mysteries from the Lord's breast. He it was who, after drinking from the Lord's breast, uttered[12] his divinity: *In the beginning was the Word, and the Word was with God.* Such a man as he was, he didn't say, "You have an advocate with the Father," but, *If anyone sins*, he said, *we have an advocate.* He didn't say, "You have" or "You have me" or "You have Christ himself," but he also

---

11. Here, as in V,9, Augustine uses the Latin propitiator, or "propitiator," but when referring to and quoting the same passage in 8 below he uses *propitiatio*, or "propitiation."

12. "Uttered": *ructavit.* The word goes well with the image of drinking, since it also means "belched."

mentioned Christ, not himself, and he said, *We have*, not "You have." He preferred to number himself among the sinners, so that he would have Christ as his advocate, rather than to put himself as an advocate instead of Christ and to be found among the proud who are to be condemned. Brothers, as an advocate with the Father we have Jesus Christ himself, the righteous one; he himself is the propitiation for our sins. He who has held onto him has caused no heresy; he who has held onto him has caused no schism. For how is it that heresies have come about?[13] When people say, "*We* are righteous." When people say, "*We* sanctify the unclean, *we* cause the wicked to be righteous, *we* petition, *we* obtain." But what did John say? *If anyone sins, we have an advocate with the Father, Jesus Christ the righteous.* Suppose someone says, "Don't the saints, then, petition on our behalf? Don't bishops and leaders,[14] then, petition on behalf of the people?" But pay attention to the scriptures and see that even leaders commend themselves to the people. For the Apostle says to the people, *Praying likewise also on our behalf* (Col 4:3). The Apostle prays on behalf of the people, the people pray on behalf of the Apostle. We pray on behalf of you, brothers, but you yourselves pray as well on behalf of us. All the members pray mutually on behalf of each other; the head intercedes for all. Hence what follows here is not surprising, and it shuts the mouths of those who cause divisions in God's Church. For he who said, *We have Jesus Christ the righteous, and he is the propitiation for our sins,* immediately added *not only ours but also the whole world's* (2:2) on account of those who were going to cause divisions and who were going to say, *See, here is Christ; see, there he is* (Mt 24:23), and who would want to give a partial view of him who bought the whole and possesses the whole. What does this mean, brothers? Certainly this: *We have found it in the fields of the woodland pastures* (Ps 132:6), we have found the Church in all nations. See, Christ *is the propitiation for our sins, not only ours but also the whole world's.* See, you have the Church everywhere in the world; don't follow false righ-

---

13. Augustine is referring to the Donatists in the remainder of this section, as is clear when he alludes to the schismatics' claim to a unique holiness, to the need to pray for bishops and priests, and to the universality of the Church. The schismatic Donatists claimed such holiness, demanded moral perfection in the hierarchy, and were geographically limited to North Africa.

14. "Bishops and leaders": *episcopi et praepositi. Praepositi* are persons set over others, and in this context they are leaders of the Church, such as apostles.

teous-makers and true off-cutters. Be upon that mountain which has filled the whole earth,[15] because Christ *is the propitiation for our sins, not only ours but also the whole world's*, which he purchased with his blood.

9. *And*, [John] says, *this is how we know him, if we keep his commandments* (2:3). Which commandments? *He who says that he knows him and does not keep his commandments is a liar, and in him there is no truth* (2:4). Yet you are still asking, "Which commandments?" *But he who keeps his word*, he says, *truly in him the love of God has been made perfect* (2:5). Let us see whether this very commandment may be called love. For we were looking for the commandments in question, and he said, *But he who keeps his word, truly in him the love of God has been made perfect*. Pay heed to the gospel as to whether this is not the commandment: *I give you a new commandment*, he says, *that you love one another* (Jn 13:34). *This is how we know that we are in him, if we have been made perfect in him* (2:5). [John] is speaking of those who are perfect in love. What is perfection in love? To love even one's enemies, and to love them to the degree that they may be brothers. For our love must not be fleshly. It is good to wish someone temporal wellbeing, but, even if that is missing, the soul is safe. Do you wish life for some friend of yours? You are doing something good. Do you rejoice at your enemy's death? You are doing something bad. But perhaps even the life that you wish for your friend is without benefit, and the death over which you are rejoicing has been beneficial for your enemy. It is uncertain whether this life is beneficial or without benefit for a particular individual, but the life that is with God is certainly beneficial. Love your enemies in such a way that you wish them to be brothers; love your enemies in such a way that they are brought into your fellowship. For that is how he loved who, as he hung on the cross, said, *Father, forgive them, because they do not know what they are doing* (Lk 23:34). For he didn't say, "Father, let these people live a long time; they are killing me, to be sure, but let them live." But what did he say? *Forgive them, because they do not know what they are doing.* By his most merciful prayer and his most extraordinary power he drove everlasting death from them. Many of them believed, and the shedding of Christ's blood was forgiven them. At first,

---

15. See Dn 2:35. The mountain is the Church, which fills the whole earth. See also 13 below and note 24.

when they were raging, they poured it out; then, when they believed, they drank it.[16] *This is how we know that we are in him, if we have been made perfect in him.* In a tone of admonition the Lord says about this very perfection of loving one's enemies, *Be perfect yourselves, therefore, as your heavenly Father is perfect* (Mt 5:48).

He who says that he abides in him, therefore, *must himself also walk as he walked* (2:6). How, brothers? What is [John] teaching us? *He who says that he abides in him*—that is, in Christ—*must himself also walk as he walked.* Is he perhaps teaching us this, that we should walk on the sea? By no means. This, then: that we should walk in the way of righteousness. In what way? I have already mentioned it. He was fastened to the cross, and he walked in that very way: it is the way of charity. *Father, forgive them, because they do not know what they are doing.* Accordingly, if you have learned to pray for your enemy, you are walking in the way of the Lord.

10. *Beloved, I am not writing you a new commandment but an old commandment, which you had from the beginning* (2:7). What did [John] say was the old commandment? *Which you had,* he says, *from the beginning.* It is old, then, because you have already heard it. Otherwise it will contradict the Lord, where he said, *I give you a new commandment, that you love one another.* But why an old commandment? Not because it pertains to the old man. But why? *Which you had from the beginning. The old commandment is the word that you have heard.* (2:7) It is old, then, because you have heard it. And he brings forth the very same new one when he says, *On the other hand I am writing you a new commandment* (2:8). Not another one, but the very same one that he referred to as old is also new. Why? *Which is true in him and in you* (2:8). You have already heard why it is old; it is because you already knew it. But why is it new? *Because the darkness has passed away, and the true light now shines* (2:8). See why it is new: because darkness pertains to the old man and light to the new. What does the apostle Paul say? *Put off the old man and put on the new* (Col 3:9-10). And what else does he say? *You were once darkness, but now you are light in the Lord* (Eph 5:8).

---

16. The allusion is to the cup of the eucharist. See also VIII,10.

11. *He who says that he is in the light* (now [John] is clarifying every-thing that he said)—*He who says that he is in the light and hates his brother is in darkness even yet* (2:9). Come now, my brothers, how long have we been telling you, *Love your enemies* (Mt 5:44)? See how much worse it is if you still hate your brothers. If you only love your brothers, you aren't yet perfect. But if you hate your brothers, what are you? Where are you? Let each one examine his own heart. He shouldn't bear hatred towards his brother because of some hard word, because of some earthly argument, lest he become earth. For whoever hates his brother may not say that he walks in the light. What did I say? He may not say that he walks in Christ. *He who says that he is in the light and hates his brother is in darkness even yet.*

Now there was some pagan or other who became a Christian. Listen to this: He was in the darkness when he was a pagan; now he has become a Christian. "Thanks be to God," everyone congratulates him. The Apostle is read in a congratulatory mood: *You were once darkness, but now you are light in the Lord.* He used to adore idols; now he adores God. He used to adore the things that he made;[17] now he adores the one who made him. He has changed. "Thanks be to God," all the Christians congratulate him. Why? Because now he is an adorer of the Father and the Son and the Holy Spirit and a detester of demons and idols. Still John is concerned about this; still he mistrusts the many congratulators. Brothers, let us willingly embrace his maternal concern. Not without reason is a mother concerned on our behalf, while others are congratulatory. I refer to charity as a mother, for she dwelled in John's heart when he said these things. Why, if not that he is fearful about something in us at the very moment when people are congratulating us? What causes him to fear? *He who says that he is in the light*—what does that mean? he who says that he is already a Chris-tian—*and hates his brother is in darkness even yet.* There is nothing to explain here, only to rejoice at or to mourn over.

12. *He who loves his brother abides in the light, and there is no scandal in him* (2:10). I beseech you by Christ. It is God who feeds us; we are about

---

17. The Latin simply has *fecit,* but Augustine probably means God and not the former pagan as the maker here.

to refresh our bodies in the name of Christ,[18] and to some degree they have been refreshed and must be refreshed. Let our mind be fed. I don't say that I am going to speak at length, for, see, the reading is now coming to an end. But if perhaps we are less [attentive] because of fatigue, let us listen attentively to what is most necessary.

He who loves his brother abides in the light, and there is no scandal in him. Who are those who suffer scandal or cause it? Those who are scandalized by Christ and by the Church. Those who are scandalized by Christ are as though burned by the sun, and those by the Church as though burned by the moon.[19] But there is a psalm that says, *The sun shall not burn you by day, nor the moon by night* (Ps 121:6), which means that, if you have maintained charity, you shall suffer scandal neither from Christ nor from the Church; you shall abandon neither Christ nor the Church. For how is he in Christ who abandons the Church and who isn't among Christ's members? Those who abandon Christ or the Church are the ones who suffer scandal, then. How do we know, when the psalm says, *The sun shall not burn you by day, nor the moon by night*, that it intends this burning scandal to be understood? Pay heed, first of all, to the similitude. Just as he who is burning says, "I can't bear it, I can't put up with it," and draws back, in the same way those who cannot bear some things in the Church and draw back from the name of Christ or from the Church are the ones who suffer scandal.

For see how scandal was suffered as though from the sun by those fleshly people to whom Christ preached about his flesh and to whom he said, *He who does not eat the flesh of the Son of Man and drink his blood shall not have life in himself* (Jn 6:53). Nearly seventy men[20] said, *These are hard words* (Jn 6:60), and they left him, and twelve remained. The sun burned all of the former, and they left, being unable to bear the force

---

18. Augustine seems to be referring to the fact that his listeners are soon going to leave the church to eat supper.

19. On the symbolism of Christ as the sun and of the Church as the moon see Hugo Rahner, *Greek Myths and Christian Mystery*, trans. Brian Battershaw (New York: Harper and Row, 1957), "The Christian Mystery of Sun and Moon," 89-176.

20. Since Jn 6:60 refers to those who left Christ as being his followers, Augustine assumes that they are identical with (according to a variant reading) the seventy disciples who are mentioned in Lk 10:1.

of his words. Twelve remained, then. And—lest perhaps people think that they themselves are benefiting Christ by believing in Christ, rather than that a benefit is being conferred on them—although the twelve remained, the Lord said to them, *Do you also want to go?* (Jn 6:67) Thus you are to know that I am indispensable to you, not you to me. But those whom the sun had not burned responded in Peter's voice, *Lord, you have the word of eternal life. To whom shall we go?* (Jn 6:68)

But whom does the Church burn as though it were the moon by night? Those who have caused schisms. Listen to the very words of the Apostle: *Who is weak and I am not weak? Who is scandalized and I do not burn?* (2 Cor 11:29) How, then, is there no scandal in him who loves his brother? Because he who loves his brother tolerates everything for the sake of unity, because brotherly love exists in the unity of charity. Someone or other offends you, whether he is evil or you think that he is evil or you imagine him as evil, and you leave so many good people! What kind of brotherly love is this? What kind has been evident in these persons?[21] While accusing Africans,[22] they have abandoned the whole world. Weren't there holy persons throughout the world? Were they able to be condemned by you unheard? But O, if you loved the brothers, there would be no scandal in you. Listen to the psalm that says, *There is great peace for those who love your law and no scandal for them* (Ps 119:165). It said that there was great peace for those who love God's law and hence no scandal for them. Those who suffer scandal, then, lose their peace. And who did it say didn't suffer scandal or cause it? Those who love God's law. They have been fixed, therefore, in charity. But someone says, "It said 'to those who love God's law,' not 'their brothers.'" Listen to what the Lord says: *I give you a new commandment, that you love one another.* What is a law if not a commandment? And how won't they suffer scandal unless they put up with each other? As Paul says, *Putting up with one another in love, striving to maintain the unity of the Spirit in*

---

21. Augustine has been speaking of the Donatists, as becomes clear in the following sentence, where he refers to Africans and contrasts Africa with the "whole world"; Donatism existed almost exclusively in Africa. He mentions them by name at the very end of the homily.

22. Augustine is referring to events of the early fourth century in Carthage, when accusations were made as to the fidelity of certain Catholic officials during a time of persecution. The raising of those accusations ultimately led to the Donatist schism.

the bond of peace (Eph 4:2-3). And, inasmuch as that itself is Christ's law, listen to the same Apostle as he commends that very law: *Bear one another's burdens,* he says, *and thus you will fulfill the law of Christ* (Gal 6:2).

13. *For he who hates his brother is in darkness, and he walks in darkness and does not know where he is going.* This is an important matter, brothers. Listen, we beg you. *He who hates his brother is in darkness, and he walks in darkness and does not know where he is going, because the darkness has blinded his eyes* (2:11). What is so blind as those who hate their brothers? For, so that you would know that they are blind, they have stumbled against a mountain. I tell you the same things so that they may not fall against you. Isn't Christ, who apart from sexual intercourse is from the kingdom of the Jews,[23] the stone that was broken off from the mountain without hands? Didn't that stone break up all the kingdoms of the earth—that is, all the ruling powers of the idols and demons? Didn't that stone grow in size and become a great mountain and fill the whole world?[24] Do we point out this mountain as the moon's third day is pointed out to people? For example, when people want to see the new moon they say, "Look at the moon! Look, that's where it is!" And if there are some there whose vision is impaired, and they say, "Where?" it is pointed out to them so that they may see it. Occasionally, when people are ashamed to be thought blind, they say that they have seen what they haven't seen. Is that how we show the Church, my brothers? Isn't it clear? Isn't it evident? Hasn't it held all nations? Isn't there fulfilled what so many years ago was promised to Abraham, that in his seed all nations would be blessed?[25] The promise was made to one man of faith, and the world has been filled with thousands of faithful persons. See the mountain filling the entire surface of the earth. See the city of which it was said: *A city set*

---

23. "Apart from sexual intercourse": *sine opere maritali.* I.e., Christ was a member of the Jewish people in every respect apart from having been sexually conceived.
24. See Dn 2:34-35. Augustine frequently uses Daniel's image of the stone that has grown into a mountain to symbolize Christ. In its having broken off from the mountain without the intervention of human hands it suggests his virginal conception: see, e.g., *Exposition I of Psalm* 101,1. In its growth into a great mountain that fills the world, however, it felicitously symbolizes the Church in its universality: see, e.g., *Exposition of Psalm* 57,9. See also III,6.
25. See Gn 22:18.

upon a mountain cannot be hidden (Mt 5:14). But there are those who stumble against the mountain. And when it is said to them, "Go up," they say, "It isn't a mountain," and it is easier for them to be dashed against its surface than to seek to live there. Yesterday Isaiah was read. Whoever of you was paying attention not only with his eyes but with his ears—not with the ears of the body but with the ears of the heart—heard: *In the last days the mountain of the house of the Lord shall be made manifest, prepared on the peak of the mountains* (Is 2:2).[26] What is as manifest as a mountain? But there are unknown mountains as well, because they are situated in one part of the earth. Which one of you is familiar with Mount Olympus? Just as those who live there don't know our Mount Giddabam. Those mountains are in different places. But that mountain is not the same, because it has filled the whole surface of the earth, and it is said of it: *Prepared on the peak of the mountains.* It is a mountain higher than the peaks of all the mountains. *And all the nations,* it says, *shall be gathered to it* (Is 2:2). Who goes astray on this mountain? Who breaks his head by stumbling against it? Who is unaware of the city set upon a mountain? But don't be surprised that it is unknown to those who hate their brothers, because they walk in darkness and don't know where they are going, because the darkness has blinded their eyes. They don't see the mountain. I don't want you to be surprised: they don't have eyes. Why don't they have eyes? Because the darkness has blinded them. How do we prove this? Because they hate their brothers. Because, when they are offended by Africans, they separate themselves from the whole world. Because they don't put up, for the sake of Christ's peace, with those whom they defame, while they do put up, for the sake of the Donatist party, with those whom they condemn.[27]

---

26. If, as is credibly argued in Poque 229, this homily was given on Easter evening, then the passage from Isaiah would have been read at the Easter Vigil, and "whoever of you was paying attention" (*quisquis vestrum vigilabat*) could just as well be translated, with Rettig, as "whoever of you was in attendance at the vigil service."

27. Augustine seems to mean that, whereas Donatists could not tolerate Catholics, they would willingly tolerate their own dissident offshoots (the most notable being the Maximianists, named after Maximian, a deacon who broke away from the main body of Donatism) for the sake of the movement as a whole.

Second Homily

1. For our instruction and salvation we should listen intently to everything that is read from the sacred scriptures. Yet the things that we should especially remember are those that have a powerful effect against heretics, whose traps are always set for weaker and less attentive persons. Recall our Lord and savior Jesus Christ and the fact that he died and rose for us—that he died because of our offenses and rose to make us righteous.[1]

Just a short while ago, in fact, you heard that he met two disciples on the road and that their eyes were closed so that they wouldn't recognize him.[2] He found them despairing of the redemption that was in Christ and believing that he had already suffered and died like a man—not thinking that, as the Son of God, he was alive forever—and that he had died in the flesh in such a way that he wouldn't return to life, just like one of the prophets. You who were attentive listened to those words a little while ago. Then he opened the scriptures to them, beginning with Moses through all the prophets, showing them that everything that he suffered had been predicted, lest they be more shaken if the Lord had risen and less believing if these things hadn't previously been said of him. Faith is firmly established by the fact that everything that happened to Christ was predicted. The disciples didn't recognize him, then, until the breaking of bread. And, to be sure, he who doesn't eat and drink to his own judgment recognizes Christ in the breaking of bread.[3]

Afterwards, also, the Eleven thought that they were seeing a ghost. He who presented himself to be crucified presented himself to be touched —crucified by his enemies, touched by his friends. Yet he is the physician of all, even of the impious, even of unbelievers. For, when the Acts of the Apostles was being read, you heard how many thousands of

---

1. See Rom 4:25.
2. See Lk 24:13-49. Poque 228-229 says that this was a reading for Easter Monday; hence this sermon would have been given on Monday evening. See Rettig's note.
3. See 1 Cor 11:29.

Christ's killers believed.[4] If those who had killed him believed afterwards, weren't those who experienced some doubt going to believe?

Now this is something that you must pay particular attention to and commit to your memory, because God wanted to raise a foundation in the scriptures (which no one who would in any way want to be identified as a Christian dares to contradict) against insidious errors: Although he even offered himself to be touched by them, this wasn't enough for him unless he also strengthened believers' hearts by way of the scriptures. For he was looking forward to us who were to come, since we have nothing to touch but *do* have something to read. For if *they* believed because they held him and touched him, what shall *we* do? Christ has ascended into heaven and isn't going to return until the end, in order to judge the living and the dead. What was going to be the basis of our belief if not the very thing whereby he wanted those who were touching him to be strengthened? So he opened the scriptures to them and showed them that Christ had to suffer and that everything that was written about him in the law of Moses and the prophets and the psalms was fulfilled; he surveyed the entire Old Testament. Whatever pertains to those scriptures proclaims Christ—but only if there are ears to listen to it. And he opened its meaning to them so that they would understand the scriptures. Hence we ourselves must pray that he may open our minds.[5]

2. But what did the Lord show was written about him in the law of Moses and the prophets and the psalms? What did he show? Let him tell us himself. The evangelist laid it out briefly so that we would know what we should believe and understand in the great breadth of the scriptures. There are indeed many pages and many books, and all of them have what the Lord said briefly to his disciples. What is that? That Christ had to suffer and rise on the third day. You have it now from the bridegroom that Christ had to suffer and rise. The bridegroom has been commended to us. Let us see what is said about the bride, so that, when you are acquainted with the bridegroom and the bride, you may appropriately attend their wedding, for every celebration is a celebration of marriage: it

---

4. See Acts 2:41. A section from the beginning of Acts had been read in the morning, along with Lk 24:13-49.
5. "Meaning ... minds": *sensum ... sensum.*

is the Church's marriage that is celebrated. The king's son is about to marry, and the king's son is himself a king and those who attend are themselves the bride. It's not the same as in fleshly weddings, where those who attend the wedding and she who is marrying are different; in the Church those who attend, if they attend well, become the bride. For the whole Church is the bride of Christ, whose origin and firstfruits are the flesh of Christ: there the bride is joined to her bridegroom in the flesh. Rightly, when he was mentioning this very flesh, did he break bread, and rightly were the eyes of his disciples opened, and they recognized him in the breaking of bread.

What, then, did the Lord say was written about him in the law and the prophets and the psalms? That Christ had to suffer. If "and rise" were not added, those whose eyes were closed would have had good reason to lament, but it was also predicted that he would rise. What was the purpose of this? Why did Christ have to suffer and rise? Because of the psalm that we greatly emphasized when we spoke of it with you on Wednesday of last week, at the first station.[6] Why did Christ have to suffer and rise? This is why: *All the ends of the earth shall remember and shall turn to the Lord, and all the lands of the nations shall adore in his presence* (Ps 22:27). Thus you may know that Christ had to suffer and rise. And what did he add here, so that after referring to the bridegroom he would also refer to the bride? *That in his name penitence and the remission of sins*, he said, *would be preached among all the nations, beginning from Jerusalem* (Lk 24:47).

You have listened, brothers; now understand. Let no one doubt that the Church is in all the nations. Let no one doubt that it began from Jerusalem and filled all the nations. We recognize the field where the vine was planted, but once it has grown we don't recognize it because it occupies it completely. Where did it begin? *From Jerusalem.* How far has it gone? *To all the nations* (Lk 24:47). There are a few that have remained; it shall have them all. In the meantime, while it is taking them all in, the farmer has caught sight of some useless branches that must be cut off;

---

6. The previous week would have been the week before Easter. The meaning of the Latin *statio* here seems to be "assembly," which is one of many possible usages of the word.

heresies and schisms have made them that way. Don't let those that have been cut off lead you astray, so that you are cut off. Instead, urge those that have been cut off to re-insert themselves once more. That Christ suffered, rose and ascended into heaven has been made manifest, and the Church too has been made manifest, because in his name penitence and the remission of sins is being preached among all the nations. Where did it begin? *Beginning from Jerusalem.* It is a person who is foolish, vain and (what more can I say?) blind who doesn't see such a vast mountain,[7] who closes his eyes against the lamp placed on the lampstand.[8]

3. When we say to them, "If you are Catholic Christians,[9] be in communion with that Church from which the gospel is spread throughout the world." When we say to them, "Be in communion with that Jerusalem,"[10] they respond to us: "We aren't in communion with that city where our king was killed, where our Lord was killed," as though they hate the city where our Lord was killed. The Jews killed him whom they found on the earth, they disdain[11] him who is seated in heaven. Who are worse—those who scorned him because they considered him a man, or those who disdain the sacraments[12] of him whom they actually confess to be God? But, indeed, they hate the city in which their own Lord was killed. Devout and merciful persons that they are, they greatly lament the fact that Christ was killed, and they kill Christ in other people! But he loved that city, and he pitied it; it was from there that he said that his preaching would begin: *Beginning from Jerusalem.* It was there that he started the preaching of his name, and you are horrified at being in communion with that city! It isn't surprising that, since you have been cut off, you hate the root. But what did he say to his disciples? *Stay in the city, because I am sending my promise to you* (Lk 24:49). See how they hate the city! Perhaps they would love it if the

---

7. See Dn 2:35.
8. See Mt 5:15.
9. I.e., not simply Christians but Catholic Christians (as opposed to the Donatist Christians who are being spoken of here). It was Augustine who helped to make this qualification famous.
10. As a note in Browne's translation remarks, Augustine seems to use "Jerusalem" as a title for the Church, although at other times he appears to be referring to the city itself. On the flexible significance of Jerusalem see John Cassian, *Conferences* XIV, 8.
11. "Disdain": *exsufflant*, literally, "blow out at," which is an expression of contempt and rejection. The term reappears in the following sentence.
12. The Donatists considered the sacraments of the Catholic Church, particularly baptism, to be invalid.

Jews who slew Christ were living in it. For, as we know, all the Christ-slayers—that is, the Jews—have been expelled from that city.[13] What it had when they were raging against Christ it has now that they are adoring Christ. Therefore they hate it because there are Christians in it. There it was that he wished to place his disciples and to send the Holy Spirit upon them. Where did the Church begin if not where the Holy Spirit came down from heaven and filled the hundred and twenty that were staying in one place? The number twelve was multiplied ten times.[14] A hundred and twenty people were staying there, and the Holy Spirit came and filled the whole place, and there was a sound like the rushing of a mighty wind, and there was something like tongues of flame divided.[15] You have heard the Acts of the Apostles. Today[16] this is the reading that was read: *They began to speak in tongues as the Holy Spirit gave them to utter* (Acts 2:4). And all who were there, Jews coming from different nations, each recognized his own tongue, and they marveled at the fact that simple and unschooled men had learned not one or two tongues but those of absolutely all the nations.[17] Where all those tongues were sounding, then, all the tongues that were going to believe were being displayed. But those who greatly love Christ, and consequently don't wish to be in communion with the city that slew Christ, honor Christ by saying that he confined himself to two tongues, Latin and Punic—that is, African. Does Christ speak only two tongues? For those are the only two tongues in the party of Donatus;[18] they have no more.

Let us be alert, brothers; let us rather look to the gift of the Spirit of God, and let us believe the things that were said previously about him, and let us see how what was said previously in the psalm has been fulfilled: *There are no languages or discourses whose voices are not heard* (Ps 19:3). And lest

---

13. The Jews were first expelled from Jerusalem by Hadrian in 135, following an uprising. After a period of relaxation, Hadrian's strictures were enforced toward the beginning of the fourth century during the reign of Constantine. Among numerous other witnesses to the Jews' expulsion, see Eusebius, *Ecclesiastical History* IV,6.
14. This throwaway sentence hints at Augustine's fascination with numbers, the basis of which is evident in *Teaching Christianity* II,16,25; *The Trinity* IV,6,10.
15. See Acts 1:15; 2:1-4.
16. I.e., in the morning.
17. See Acts 2:5-13.
18. "In the party of Donatus": in parte *Donati*. Augustine typically refers to the Donatists as the party of Donatus, the fourth-century bishop of Carthage after whom Donatism took its name, thus emphasizing their sectionalism in contrast to the universal quality of the Catholic Church.

anyone think that those tongues themselves came to one place rather than that Christ's gift came to all those tongues, listen to what comes next: *Their sound went forth through all the earth, and their words to the ends of the world* (Ps 19:4). Why is this so? *Because he pitched his tent in the sun* (Ps 19:4)—that is, in the open. His tent is his flesh; his tent is his Church. It was pitched in the sun; it isn't in the night but in the day. But why don't they recognize it? Go back to the reading that was finished yesterday and see why they don't recognize it: *He who hates his brother walks in darkness and does not know where he is going, because the darkness has blinded his eyes* (2:11).[19] Let us, then, look at what follows, and let us not be in darkness. How shall we not be in darkness? If we love the brothers. What proof is there that we love the brotherhood? That we don't sever its unity, because we maintain charity.

4. *I am writing to you, little children, because your sins are forgiven through his name* (2:12). Therefore, little children, you are born through the forgiveness of your sins. But through whose name are your sins forgiven? Through that of Augustine? Then not through the name of Donatus either. You see who Augustine is and who Donatus is. Nor through Paul's name or Peter's name either. For, to those who are dividing the Church and attempting to fracture its unity, the childbearing mother charity in the Apostle manifests her heart, in a certain sense rends her womb with her words, beseeches the children whom she sees being carried away, recalls to the one name those desirous of making many names for themselves, turns them away from loving her so that they may love Christ, and says, *Was Paul crucified for you? Or were you baptized in Paul's name?* (1 Cor 1:13) What is he saying? I don't want for you to be mine but for you to be with me. Be with me! We all belong to him who died for us, who was crucified for us, which is why it says, *Your sins are forgiven through his name*, not through anyone else's.

5. *I am writing to you, fathers* (2:13). Why first sons? *Because your sins are forgiven through his name*, and you are reborn into new life: therefore sons. Why fathers? *Because you have known him who is from the beginning* (2:13), for beginning pertains to fatherhood. Christ is new in the flesh

---

19. This version of the verse is slightly different from the version that appears in I,13 and in V,7.

but ancient in divinity.[20] How ancient do we think? How many years old? Do we think that he is older than his mother? Obviously he is older than his mother, *for everything was made through him* (Jn 1:3). If everything, then in his ancientness he even made his mother herself, from whom in his newness he was born. Do we think before his mother alone? He was ancient even before his mother's ancestors. His mother's ancestor was Abraham, and the Lord says, *Before Abraham I am* (Jn 8:58). Are we saying before Abraham? Before man existed heaven and earth were made. Before them there was—or rather *is*—the Lord. For it was very correctly not said, "Before Abraham I was," but, *Before Abraham I am*. For, when it is said that something was, it is not [now], and when it is said that something will be, it is not yet.[21] He knows nothing else than being. Inasmuch as God is, he knows being; he knows nothing of having been and of being about to be. There is one day there, but it is forever. Yesterday and tomorrow don't situate that day between themselves, for, once yesterday is finished, the today that is starting will be finished by the coming tomorrow. That one day there is without darkness, without night, without place, without measure, without hours. Say what you want it to be: if you wish, it is a day; if you wish, it is a year; if you wish, it is years. For it has been said of it: *And your years shall not fail* (Ps 102:27). But when has it been called a day? When it was said by the Lord: *Today I have begotten you* (Ps 2:7). Begotten by the eternal Father, begotten from eternity, begotten in eternity,[22] with no beginning, with no end, with no length of space, because he is what is, because he himself is he who is. He spoke this very name of his to Moses: *You shall tell them: He who is sent me to you* (Ex 3:14). What, then, was before Abraham? What was before Noah? What was before Adam? Listen to scripture: *Before the daystar I begot you* (Ps 110:3). Finally, before heaven and earth. Why? Because *everything was made through him, and apart*

---

20. From here until the end of the present section Augustine is probably envisaging the position of the Arians, who denied the full divinity of Christ. Augustine is arguing for the Son's eternal origin, which was disputed by the Arians, and his selection of scriptural passages—especially Pss. 2:7; 110:3; Jn 1:3—is chosen from the anti-Arian arsenal that was typically used by early Christian writers. The Arians are mentioned briefly by name, with other heretics, in VI,12.
21. See *Confessions* XI,14,17-22,28.
22. "By ... from ... in": *ab ... ex ... in.*

from him nothing was made (Jn 1:3). Recognize the fathers, then. For they become fathers by recognizing what is from the beginning.

6. *I am writing to you, young men* (2:13). There are sons, there are fathers, there are young men—sons because they are born, fathers because they recognize the beginning, but why young men? *Because you have conquered the evil one* (2:13). In the sons there is birth, in the fathers there is ancientness, in the young men there is strength. If the evil one is conquered by young men, [it means that] he fights with us. He fights but doesn't overcome.[23] Why? Because we are strong? Or because he is strong in us who was found to be weak in the hands of his persecutors? He who didn't resist his persecutors has made us strong. For he was crucified out of weakness, but he lives by the power of God.[24]

7. *I am writing to you, children* (2:14). Why children? *Because you have known the Father* (2:14). [John] commends this and repeats, *Because you have known him who is from the beginning* (2:14). Remember that you are fathers. If you forget him who is from the beginning, you have lost your fatherhood. *I am writing to you, young men.* Consider again and again that you are young men: fight so as to conquer, conquer so as to be crowned, be humble so as not to fall in the fight. *I am writing to you, young men, because you are strong, and the word of God abides in you, and you have conquered the evil one* (2:14).

8. All of these things, brothers—that we know what is from the beginning, that we are strong, that we know the Father: they commend all of these things as knowledge. They don't commend charity.[25] If we know, we should love, for knowledge apart from charity doesn't save. *Knowledge puffs up, charity builds up* (1 Cor 8:1). If you wish to confess and not to love, you are beginning to be like the demons. Demons were in the habit of confessing the Son of God, and they would say, *What is that to us and to you?* (Mt 8:29) And they were driven out. Confess and embrace. For they were afraid because of their wickedness, but you must love the one who forgives your wickedness.

---

23. "Fights ... fights ... overcome": *pugnat ... pugnat ... expugnat.*
24. See 2 Cor 13:4.
25. These are undoubtedly the Donatists.

But how shall we be able to love God if we love the world? [John] prepares us, therefore, to be inhabited by charity. There are two loves, that of the world and that of God.[26] If love of the world dwells in us, there is no way for the love of God to enter in. Let love of the world·withdraw and that of God dwell in us; what is better should take its place. You used to love the world; don't love the world [now]. When you have emptied your heart of earthly love, you will draw in divine love, and thereupon charity begins to dwell in you, from which nothing evil can proceed. Listen, therefore, to the words of the one who is now cleansing you. He finds the hearts of men to be like a field. And how does he find them? If he finds growth there, he destroys it; if he finds the field cleared, he plants. He wants to plant the tree of charity there. And what growth does he want to destroy? Love of the world. Listen to the destroyer of the growth. *Do not love the world*—for this is what follows—*nor those things that are in the world. If anyone loves the world, the love of the Father is not in him.* (2:15)

9. You have heard that *if anyone loves the world, the love of the Father is not in him.* Brothers, lest anyone say in his heart that this is false, God says (it is the Holy Spirit who spoke through the Apostle) that nothing is more true: *If anyone loves the world, the love of the Father is not in him.* Do you want to have the Father's love so that you may be the Son's co-heirs? Don't love the world. Shut out the evil love of the world so that you may be filled with the love of God. You are a vessel, but you are still full. Pour out what you have so that you may receive what you don't have. To be sure, our brothers have now been reborn from water and the Holy Spirit, and we were reborn some years ago from water and the Spirit. It is good for us not to love the world, lest the sacraments remain in us to our condemnation, not as supports to our salvation. It is a support to our salvation to have the root of charity, to have the strength of piety, not only its appearance. The appearance is good, the appearance is holy, but of what use is the appearance if it isn't attached to the root? Isn't a branch that has been cut off thrown into the fire? It has an appearance, but in the root. How are you rooted so that you may not be uprooted? By holding onto charity. As the apostle Paul says, *Rooted and supported in charity* (Eph 3:17). How will

---

26. Augustine most famously elaborates on these two loves in *The City of God* XIV,28.

charity be rooted in the midst of all the growth of the love of the world? Destroy the growth. You are about to be placed as a great seed; let there be nothing in the field that might smother the seed. These are the destroying words that [John] spoke: *Do not love the world, nor those things that are in the world. If anyone loves the world, the charity of the Father is not in him.*

10. *Because all the things that are in the world are the desire of the flesh and the desire of the eyes and the ambition of the world* (he mentioned three things), *which are not from the Father but are from the world. And the world is passing away, along with its desires. But he who does the will of God abides forever, just as he himself also abides forever.* (2:16-17)

Why wouldn't you love what God made? Which do you want, to love temporal things and to pass away with time or not to love the world and to live forever with God? The stream of temporal things draws on, but our Lord Jesus Christ is like a tree that has been born beside a stream.[27] He took on flesh, died, rose, ascended into heaven. He wanted to plant himself in some way beside the river of temporal things. Are you being rushed headlong? Hold onto the wood. Has love of the world disoriented you? Hold onto Christ. For your sake he became temporal so that you might become eternal, because he also became temporal in such a way as to remain eternal. Something of time was added to him, nothing of eternity was withdrawn. But you were born temporal, and through sin you became temporal. You became temporal through sin, he became temporal through the mercy of forgiving sins. What is the difference, when two people are in a prison, between the criminal and his visitor? For a person sometimes comes to his friend and goes in to visit him, and both seem to be in prison, but they are very different and distinct from one another: the one's situation burdens him, the other's kindness drew him [there]. Thus we were being held by our guilt in this mortal condition. In his mercy he came down. He went in to the prisoner as a redeemer, not as an oppressor. The Lord poured out his blood on our behalf, he redeemed us, he transformed our hope. Yet we still bear the mortality of our flesh, and we look forward to future immortality.

---

27. See Ps 1:3.

And we are tossed about on the sea, but we have already fastened an anchor of hope on the land.

11. But let us not love the world, nor the things that are in the world. For the things that are in the world are *the desire of the flesh and the desire of the eyes and the ambition of the world.*[28] These are three things, so that no one may chance to say, "God made the things that are in the world—that is, heaven and earth, sea, sun, moon, stars, all the ornaments of heaven. What are the ornaments of the sea? All gliding things. What are those of the earth? Animals, trees, birds. They are in the world, God made them. Why, then, wouldn't I love what God made?" May the Spirit of God be in you, so that you may see that all these things are good, but woe to you if you love created things and abandon the creator. They are beautiful as far as you are concerned, but how much more beautiful is he who formed them? Let Your Charity be attentive, for you can be taught by metaphors. Don't let Satan creep up on you, saying what he customarily says: "Enjoy yourself in God's creation. Why did he make those things if not for you to enjoy them?" And they get drunk, and they ruin themselves, and they forget their creator. As long as they use created things not temperately but inordinately, the creator is disdained. Of such persons the Apostle says, *They adored and served the creature rather than the creator, who is blessed forever* (Rom 1:25). God doesn't forbid you to love those things, but you mustn't love them in the expectation of blessedness. Rather, you must favor and praise them in such a way that you love the creator.

Brothers, if a bridegroom made a ring for his bride, and she loved the ring that she had received more than her bridegroom, who made the ring, in the same way wouldn't an adulterous soul be detected in the bridegroom's very gift, even though she loved what the bridegroom gave her? To be sure, she loved what the bridegroom gave her. Yet, if she said, "This ring is enough for me; now I don't want to see his face again," what sort of person would she be? Who wouldn't detest this crazy woman? Who wouldn't convict her of an adulterous mind? You love gold instead

---

28. This begins a lengthy treatment of these three conditions. For a still lengthier treatment, in the form of an examination of conscience by Augustine, see *Confessions* X,30,41–41,66.

of the man, you love a ring instead of your bridegroom. If this is how it is with you, that you love a ring instead of your bridegroom and don't want to see your bridegroom, then he gave this earnest to you not to pledge himself to you but to keep you away from him. A bridegroom gives a pledge for the very purpose that he himself may be loved in his pledge. That is why God gave you all these things, then; love him who made them. There is more that he wants to give you—that is, himself, who made them. But if you love these things, although God made them, and you neglect the creator and love the world, won't your love be considered adulterous?

12. For the term "world" applies not only to this structure which God made—to the heavens and the earth, the sea, things visible and invisible; the inhabitants of the world are also referred to as the world, just as the term "house" refers to both its walls and its inhabitants. And sometimes we praise a house and disparage its inhabitants. For we say, "That's a good house, because it's made of marble and has beautiful paneling." And at another time we say, "That's a good house; no one there suffers any hurt, no robberies and no acts of violence take place there." Then we aren't praising the walls but those who dwell within the walls. Yet each is called a house, whether the one or the other. For all lovers of the world, because they inhabit the world by their love, just as they inhabit heaven whose hearts are above and who walk on the earth in their flesh—all lovers of the world, therefore, are referred to as "the world." They have nothing but these three things, the desire of the flesh, the desire of the eyes and the ambition of the world, for they desire to eat, to drink, to have sexual intercourse—to use these pleasures. Isn't there moderation in these things? Or, when it is said, "Don't love these things," is this said so that you won't eat or drink or beget children? It isn't for this reason that it is said. But there should be moderation on account of the creator, so that you don't encumber yourselves with this love, lest you love for the purpose of enjoying what you should possess for the purpose of using.[29] For you aren't put to the test unless two things are placed before you.

---

29. The distinction between enjoying (*frui*) and using (*uti*) is a famous one in Augustine. As he understands the terms, only God is to be enjoyed, while everything else is to be used in order to attain to God. For his most detailed explanation see *Teaching Christianity* I. Consult also

Which of the two do you want, righteousness or profit? "I don't have the means to live, I don't have the means to eat, I don't have the means to drink," [you say]. But what is the good of it if you can only have them through wickedness? Isn't it better to love what you don't lose than to engage in wickedness? You see the profit of gold, but you don't see the destruction of faith. This is what [John] says to us, then: *the desire of the flesh*—that is, the desire for the things that pertain to the flesh, like food and sexual intercourse and other such things.

13. *And the desire of the eyes.* He calls all curiosity the desire of the eyes. How extensive is curiosity? It is in spectacles, in theaters, in the devil's sacraments,[30] in magic, in evil deeds; that is where curiosity is. Occasionally it tempts even the servants of God, so that they want to perform some sort of miracle and to discover whether God will reply to their prayers with miracles. That is curiosity, that is the desire of the eyes. It is not from the Father. If God has given it, do it, for he presented it for you to do, for it isn't the case that those who haven't done it won't belong to the kingdom of God.[31] When the apostles rejoiced that the demons were subject to them, what did the Lord tell them? *Do not rejoice because of that, but rejoice because your names are written in heaven* (Lk 10:20). The reason why he wanted the apostles to rejoice is the reason why you should rejoice as well. For woe to you if your name isn't written in heaven. Woe to you if you haven't raised the dead? Woe to you if you haven't walked upon the sea? Woe to you if you haven't cast out demons? If you have received the means to do these things, use them humbly, not proudly. For the Lord said of certain pseudo-prophets that they were going to perform signs and prodigies.[32] Let there be, then, no ambition of the world. For pride is the ambition of the world—wanting to promote oneself by honors. A person seems great to himself whether because of riches or because of some power.

Raymond Canning, "*Uti/frui*," in Allan D. Fitzgerald, ed., *Augustine through the Ages* (Grand Rapids: Eerdmans, 1999) 859-861.

30. "The devil's sacraments": *sacramentis diaboli*. Augustine is probably referring here to pagan rites of worship and perhaps in particular to the rites of the mystery religions, since the Latin *sacramentum* translates the Greek *mysterion*.

31. I.e., if God has given the power to do anything, including a miracle.

32. See Mt 24:24.

14. There are these three, and apart from either the desire of the flesh or the desire of the eyes or the ambition of the world you find nothing to tempt human cupidity. It was by these three that the Lord was tempted by the devil. He was tempted by the desire of the flesh when it was said to him, *If you are the Son of God, tell these stones to become bread* (Mt 4:3), when he was hungry after fasting. But how did he repel the tempter and teach his soldier to fight? Listen to what he said to him: *Man does not live by bread alone but by God's every word* (Mt 4:4).

And he was tempted by the desire of the eyes with regard to a miracle when [the devil] told him, *Throw yourself down, because it is written: He commanded his angels concerning you that they should lift you up if your foot should ever stumble against a stone* (Mt 4:6). He resisted the tempter, for, if he performed a miracle, he would have seemed either to have given in to him or to have done it out of curiosity, for he performed them when, as God, he wanted to do so—but in order to cure the sick. If he did it then,[33] he would have seemed to have done so merely because he wanted a miracle. But, so that people wouldn't think this, listen to what he responded: *Get behind me, Satan, for it is written: You shall not tempt the Lord your God* (Mt 4:7)—that is, "If I do this, I shall be tempting God." He said this because he wanted you to say it. Suppose the enemy puts this thought in your mind, "What sort of man are you? What sort of Christian are you? Haven't you performed at least one miracle, or have the dead arisen because of your prayers, or have you healed the sick? If you were really someone important, you would perform some miracle." Then you should respond and say, "It is written: *You shall not tempt the Lord your God.* I won't tempt God, therefore, as though I would belong to God if I performed a miracle and wouldn't belong to him if I didn't. And where are his words, *Rejoice because your names are written in heaven?*"

How was the Lord tempted with respect to the ambition of the world? When [the devil] lifted him high up and said to him, *I will give you all these things if you fall down and adore me* (Mt 4:9). He wanted to tempt

---

33. I.e., at the devil's behest.

the king of the ages[34] with pride over an earthly kingdom. But the Lord who made heaven and earth spurned the devil. What great thing would it be for the devil to be conquered by the Lord? What, then, did he reply to the devil except what he has taught you to reply? *It is written: You shall adore the Lord your God, and him alone shall you serve* (Mt 4:10).

If you hold to these things you won't have the concupiscence of the world. By not having the concupiscence of the world, neither the desire of the flesh nor the desire of the eyes nor the ambition of the world will conquer you, and you will make a place for charity to enter, so that you may love God, because, if the love of the world is there, the love of God won't be there. Hold, rather, to the love of God, so that, just as God is eternal, you also may abide in eternity, because a person's love determines the person's quality. Do you love the earth? You will be earth. Do you love God? What shall I say? That you will be God? I don't dare to say this on my own. Let us listen to the scriptures: *I have said that you are gods and that all of you are sons of the Most High* (Ps 82:6). If, then, you want to be gods and sons of the Most High, *do not love the world, nor those things that are in the world. If anyone loves the world, the charity of the Father is not in him, because all the things that are in the world are the desire of the flesh and the desire of the eyes and the ambition of the world, which are not from the Father but are from the world*—that is, from the people who are lovers of the world. *And the world is passing away, along with its desires. But he who does the will of God abides forever, just as God also abides forever.*

---

34. "Ages": *saeculorum.* Some manuscripts have *caelorum* ("of the heavens"). In either case a striking contrast is established.

Third Homily

1. *Children, it is the last hour* (2:18). In this reading [John] is addressing children, so that they may grow up quickly, because it is the last hour. Bodily age is not within the will's capacity. Hence, no one grows up in terms of the flesh when he wills, just as no one is born when he wills. But when there is a birth in the will, then there is also a growing up in the will.[1] No one is born of water and the Spirit unless he wills it. If he wills it, then, he grows; if he wills it, he diminishes. What is growing? Progressing. What is diminishing? Regressing. Let whoever knows that he has been born be aware that he is a child and an infant; let him eagerly open his mouth to his mother's breasts, and he will grow quickly. Now, his mother is the Church and her breasts are the two testaments of the divine scriptures. From them is sucked the milk of all the sacraments that are performed in time for the sake of our eternal salvation so that, having been nursed and strengthened, he may arrive at the food that must be eaten, which is: *In the beginning was the Word, and the Word was with God, and the Word was God* (Jn 1:1). Our milk is the humble Christ; our food is the very same Christ, equal to the Father. He nurses you with milk so that he may feed you with bread, for to touch Jesus spiritually with the heart is to understand that he is equal to the Father.[2]

2. For this same reason he forbade Mary to touch him, and said to her, *Do not touch me, for I have not yet ascended to the Father* (Jn 20:17). What does this mean? Did he offer himself to his disciples to be touched and did he avoid contact with Mary? Wasn't it he himself who said to his doubting disciple, *Put your fingers and touch my wounds* (Jn 20:27)? Had he already ascended to the Father? Why, then, does he forbid Mary and say, *Do not touch me, for I have not yet ascended to the Father*? Is this what we should say, that he didn't fear to be touched by men but did fear to be touched by women? Touching him purifies all flesh. Did he

---

1. There is a similar thought in Gregory of Nyssa, *The Life of Moses* II,3.
2. For the metaphor of milk and solid food see also 1 Cor 3:2. Milk imagery was part of patristic baptismal symbolism: see Clement of Alexandria, *Paidagogos* I,6,35; Hippolytus, *Apostolic Tradition* 21; Ambrose, *Exposition of Psalm* 118,XVI,21.

fear to be touched by those to whom he first wanted to be manifested? Wasn't his resurrection announced first by women to men,[3] so that by an unexpected stratagem the serpent might be conquered? For, because he announced his death to the first man by a woman,[4] his life as well was announced to men by a woman. Why, then, didn't he want to be touched if not because he wanted that touching to be understood as spiritual? A spiritual touch comes from a pure heart. He touches Christ from a pure heart who understands that he is coequal with the Father. But he who doesn't yet understand the divinity of Christ goes as far as his flesh, but he doesn't go as far as his divinity. Now what is so great in arriving at the same point as did the persecutors who crucified him? The great thing is understanding that the Word, through whom all things were made, was God, with God in the beginning. That is how he wanted to be known, when he said to Philip, *As long as I have been with you, have you not known me, Philip? He who sees me also sees the Father.* (Jn 14:9)

3. But, lest there be someone who is lazy in making progress, let him listen: *Children, it is the last hour.* Make progress, run, grow: it is the last hour. This last hour is long, yet it is the last. In fact [John] used *hour* instead of "last time," because in the last times our Lord Jesus Christ will come. But some people will say, "How is this the last time? How is this the last hour? Certainly the Antichrist will come first, and then the day of judgment will come." John was aware of those thoughts. In case people were feeling somewhat secure and consequently were thinking that it wasn't the last hour and that the Antichrist was yet to come, he told them, *And just as you have heard that the Antichrist is going to come, now many antichrists have appeared* (2:18). Could there be many antichrists if it weren't the last hour?

4. Whom did he call antichrists? He continues and explains. *This is why we know that it is the last hour* (2:18). Why? *Because many antichrists have appeared. They left us.* (2:19) See the antichrists: *They left us.* Therefore we lament their loss. Listen to the consolation: *But they were not of us* (2:19). All the heretics, all the schismatics left us—that is,

---

3. See Mt 28:8 par.
4. See presumably Gn 3:14-15.

they left the Church; but they wouldn't have left if they were of us. Before they left, then, they were not of us. If they left before, they were not of us. There are many who are within; they didn't leave, and yet they are antichrists. We dare to say this: To what purpose, if not that whoever is within shouldn't be an antichrist? For [John] is about to describe and to designate the antichrists, and we shall see them now.

Each one ought to examine his own conscience as to whether he is the antichrist. For in Latin "antichrist" means "contrary to Christ." It isn't as some understand it, that the Antichrist is so called because he is going to come before Christ[5]—that is, that after him Christ is going to come. That isn't the way it is said, that isn't the way it is written; rather Antichrist —that is, contrary to Christ. Thanks to [John's] explanation you have now learned who is already contrary to Christ, and you understand that only antichrists can leave, whereas those who are not contrary to Christ can in no respect leave. For he who isn't contrary to Christ remains in his body and is considered his member. His members are never contrary to one another. The body's wholeness depends on all its members. And what does the Apostle say about the harmony of the members? *If one member suffers, all the members suffer with him, and if one member is glorified, all the members rejoice with him* (1 Cor 12:26). If in the glorifi- cation of a member, then, the other members rejoice with him, and in his suffering all the members suffer, the harmony of the members doesn't allow for an antichrist. And as those who are within are in the body of our Lord Jesus Christ, so in Christ's body there are, in a manner of speaking, evil humors,[6] inasmuch as his body is still in the process of being healed and won't be in perfect health until the resurrection of the dead. When they are vomited out, then the body finds relief; likewise, when the wicked leave, then the Church finds relief. And, when it vomits them out

---

5. "Before Christ": *ante Christum*. The Latin for "antichrist" is *antichristus*. Augustine is making a statement here solely about the literal meaning of *antichristus*—indeed, of its spelling—and is not necessarily denying that an Antichrist, acting on a larger scale than that of the individual Christian who contravenes Christ's commandments, might also arrive before Christ's second coming, which 2 Thes 2:3-10 and the second half of Rev seem to suggest.

6. The ancients understood the humors to be fluids that determined the physical and mental character of a person, depending on their proportions in the body.

and its body rejects them, it says,[7] "Those humors left me, but they were not of me." What does that mean, "They were not of me?" "They weren't cut from my flesh, but they oppressed my heart when they were in me."

5. *They left us, but*—don't be downcast—*they were not of us.* How do you know? *Because, if they had been of us, they would certainly have remained with us* (2:19). From this, then, let Your Charity be aware that there are many who are not of us. They receive the sacraments with us, they receive baptism with us, they receive with us what the faithful know that they themselves receive—the blessing, the eucharist,[8] and whatever there is in the holy sacraments. With us they share the altar itself, and they are not of us.[9] It is trial which proves that they are not of us. When trial touches them, they fly outside as though blown by the wind, because they weren't grain. But—what must frequently be stated—when the winnowing on the Lord's threshing floor begins on the day of judgment, then they will all be blown away.[10] *They left us, but they were not of us, because, if they had been of us, they would certainly have remained with us.*

Now, do you want to know, dearest, how it is said with great certainty that those who perhaps leave and return aren't antichrists, aren't contrary to Christ? It isn't possible that those who aren't antichrists would remain without. But it is of his own will that a person is either an antichrist or in Christ. We are either among his members or among the evil humors. Whoever is changed for the better is a member in his body, but whoever abides in wickedness is an evil humor and, when he leaves, those who were being oppressed will find relief. *They left us, but they were not of us, because, if they had been of us, they would certainly have remained with us. But this happened so that they would be manifested as not all being with us.* (2:19) [John] added *so that they would be manifested* because, although they are within, they are not of us; yet they aren't manifest but become manifest by leaving.

---

7. It seems to be the Church speaking here.
8. "The blessing, the eucharist": *benedictionem, eucharistiam.* Some manuscripts read *benedictionem eucharistiae* ("the blessing of the eucharist"), which perhaps makes more sense in the context.
9. Augustine is describing the Donatists here. Catholics accepted their sacraments as valid, and in that sense they shared both sacraments and altar with Catholics.
10. See Mt 3:12.

And you have an anointing from the Spirit, so that you may be mani-fested to yourselves (2:20).[11] The spiritual anointing is the Holy Spirit himself, whose sacrament is in the visible anointing.[12] [John] says that all who have this anointing of Christ recognize the good and the bad, nor is it necessary that they be taught, because the anointing itself teaches them.

6. *I am writing to you not because you do not know the truth but because you do know it, and because every lie is not of the truth* (2:21). See how we have been shown how to recognize an antichrist. What is Christ? The truth. He himself said, *I am the truth* (Jn 14:6). But *every lie is not of the truth*. All who lie, then, aren't yet of Christ. He didn't say that there was a certain lie that was of the truth and a certain lie that wasn't of the truth. Listen to the words, lest you flatter yourselves, lest you congratulate yourselves, lest you deceive yourselves, lest you mock yourselves: *Every lie is not of the truth.* Let us see, then, how the antichrists lie, because there isn't one kind of lie.

Who is the liar, if not he who denies that Jesus is the Christ? (2:22) "Jesus" has one meaning and "Christ" has another. Although Jesus Christ our savior is one, nonetheless Jesus is his proper name. Just as Moses is called by his proper name, and also Elijah and Abraham, so our Lord Jesus has a proper name. But Christ is the name of a sacrament.[13] Just as one may be called a prophet or one may be called a priest, so Christ is commended as one who has been anointed, in whom there was the redemption of the whole people of Israel. This Christ was hoped for by the people of the Jews as the one who was to come, and, because he came as humble, he wasn't recognized; because he was a small stone, they stumbled against him and were broken. But the stone grew and became a great mountain.[14] And what does scripture say? *Whoever stum-bles against this stone shall be shattered, and it shall crush the one upon*

---

11. The second half of this verse (*so that you may be manifested* ...) is not found in any manuscript of the epistle, but it looks very much as if it was part of the text that Augustine used.

12. This is the anointing that formed part of the rite of baptism, which is further discussed in 12 below. In VI,10 Augustine will also allude to the imposition of the hand, which likewise formed part of the baptismal rite and which he there associates with the gift of the Spirit.

13. This use of the term illustrates the broad meaning of "sacrament" in Christian antiquity. In the present instance "sacrament" refers to a sacred office.

14. See Dn 2:35. See also I,13 and note 23.

whom it comes (Lk 20:18). The words must be distinguished. It says that the one who stumbles shall be shattered, while the one upon whom it comes shall be crushed. Because he first came as humble, people stumbled against him; because he will come to judge as lofty, he will crush him upon whom he comes. But when he comes he won't crush him whom he didn't shatter when he came. He who didn't stumble against him when he was humble won't fear him when he is lofty. You have heard it concisely, brothers: he who didn't stumble against him when he was humble won't fear him when he is lofty. For, to all those who are wicked, Christ is a stone of stumbling; whatever Christ says is bitter to them.

7. Listen now and see. Certainly all who leave the Church and are cut off from the unity of the Church are antichrists. Let no one doubt it, for [John] himself pointed it out: *They left us, but they were not of us, for, if they had been of us, they would certainly have remained with us.* Whoever do not remain with us, then, but leave us: it is manifest that they are antichrists. And how are they proved to be antichrists? By their lying. And *who is the liar, if not he who denies that Jesus is the Christ?* Let us question the heretics. Whom do you find to be a heretic, who denies that Jesus is the Christ? Let Your Charity see a great sacrament.[15] Listen to what the Lord Jesus inspired in us and what I would like to suggest to you.

See, they left us and became Donatists. We ask them whether Jesus is the Christ; at once they confess that Jesus is the Christ. If, then, he is an antichrist who denies that Jesus is the Christ, neither can they call us antichrists nor we them, because both we and they confess. If, then, neither they call us that nor we them, then neither did they leave us nor we them. If we didn't leave ourselves, then, we are in unity. If we are in unity, why are there two altars in this city? Why are there divided houses and divided marriages? Why is there a common bed and a divided Christ? [John] warns us that he wants us to speak what is true. Either they have left us or we them. But far be it from us to have left them, for we have the testament of the Lord's inheritance. We read it and there we find: *I will give you the nations as your inheritance, and the ends of the earth as your possession* (Ps 2:8). We hold Christ's inheritance; they don't hold it.

---

15. The phrase seems to be equivalent to "Let me introduce you to a great mystery."

They aren't in communion with the world; they aren't in communion with the entire earth that has been redeemed by the blood of the Lord. We have the Lord himself, risen from the dead, who offered himself to the hands of his doubting disciples to be touched.[16] And when they still doubted him, he said to them, *Christ had to suffer and rise on the third day, and in his name penance and the remission of sins would be preached* (Lk 24:46-47). Where? In which place? To whom? *Throughout all the nations, beginning from Jerusalem* (Lk 24:27). We are sure of the unity of our inheritance. Whoever isn't in communion with this inheritance has left for elsewhere.

8. But let us not be saddened. *They left us, but they were not of us, for, if they had been of us, they would certainly have remained with us.* If they left us, then, they are antichrists. If they are antichrists, they are liars. If they are liars, they deny that Jesus is the Christ. Once again we return to the crux of the question. Ask them individually, they confess that Jesus is the Christ. The tight reasoning in this epistle constrains us. You certainly see the question. If it isn't grasped, this question is troublesome for both us and them. Either we are antichrists or they are antichrists. They call us antichrists, and they say that we left them; we say the same thing about them. But this epistle has pointed out the antichrists. Whoever denies that Jesus is the Christ, he is an antichrist. Now let us inquire who would make this denial, and let us pay attention not to words but to deeds.

For, if all are asked, all confess with one voice that Jesus is the Christ. Let the tongue be silent for a little while. Put their life to the question. If we find this out, if scripture itself tells us that this denial isn't only a matter of words but also of deeds, we certainly find many antichrists who profess Christ with their lips and differ from Christ by their behavior. Where do we find this in scripture? Listen to the apostle Paul. When he was speaking of such persons he said, *For they confess that they know God, but by their deeds they deny him* (Ti 1:16). And we also find the antichrists themselves: whoever denies Christ by his deeds is an antichrist. I pay no heed to words; I look at lives. Actions speak, and do we demand words? For what wicked person doesn't want to speak well?

---

16. See Jn 20:27.

But what does the Lord say of such persons? *Hypocrites, how can you say good things when you are wicked?* (Mt 12:34) You offer your words to my ears, but I look at your thoughts: there I see an evil will, and you display false fruits. I know what and from where I would gather: I don't gather figs from thistles, I don't gather grapes from thorns. For any tree whatsoever is known by its fruit.[17] The antichrist who with his lips professes that Jesus is the Christ and by his deeds denies it is that much more of a liar. He is a liar because he says one thing and does another.

9. Now then, brothers, if it is deeds that must be questioned, we find not only that many antichrists have left for elsewhere but that many, who haven't left for elsewhere, aren't yet manifest. However many the Church has of perjurers, cheats, sorcerers, fortune-tellers, adulterers, drunkards, money-lenders, dishonest tradesmen and all the things that we cannot number—they are contrary to the teaching of Christ, they are contrary to the Word of God. The Word of God, however, is Christ; whatever is contrary to the Word of God is in the Antichrist, for the Antichrist is contrary to Christ. Do you want to know how openly these people resist Christ? Sometimes it happens that they do something bad and begin to be corrected. Because they don't dare to blaspheme Christ, they blaspheme his ministers, by whom they are being corrected. But, if you demonstrate to them that you are speaking Christ's words and not yours, they try, as much as they can, to convict you of speaking your own words, not Christ's words. But, if it is clear that you are speaking Christ's words, they even go against Christ, they begin to rebuke Christ. "How and why," they say, "did he make us this way?" Don't people who have been convicted of their deeds say this daily? Perverted by a wicked will, they accuse their maker. Since it was the very one who made us that re-made us, their maker cries out to them from heaven, "What did I make you? I made the person, not the avarice; I made the person, not the theft; I made the person, not the adultery. You have heard that my works praise me. The very hymn from the lips of the three boys was what protected them

17. See Mt 7:16.

from the flames."[18] The works of the Lord praise the Lord. Heaven praises him, and the earth and the sea. Everything that is in heaven praises him: the angels praise him, the stars praise him, the great lights praise him. Whatever swims praises him, whatever flies, whatever walks, whatever crawls: all those things praise the Lord. Have you heard that avarice praises the Lord? Have you heard that drunkenness praises the Lord, that sensuality praises him, that foolishness praises him? The Lord didn't make whatever you don't hear of as praising the Lord there. Correct what you have done, so that what God has made[19] in you may be saved. But if you don't want this, and you love and embrace your sins, you are contrary to Christ. Whether you are within or elsewhere, you are an antichrist. Whether you are within or elsewhere, you are chaff. But why aren't you within? Because you haven't encountered the wind.[20]

10. Now these things have been manifested, brothers. Lest anyone say, "I don't worship Christ, but I worship God, his Father"—*everyone who denies the Son possesses neither the Son nor the Father, and he who confesses the Son possesses both the Son and the Father* (2:23). [John] is speaking to you as grains, and those who were chaff should listen so that they may become grains. A person should look to his conscience and, if he is a lover of the world, should be changed. Let him become a lover of Christ so that he may not be an antichrist. If someone tells him that he is an antichrist, he is angry; he considers that he has been insulted. Perhaps he threatens a lawsuit if he hears that he is an antichrist from the person with whom he is quarreling. Christ tells him, "Be patient. If you heard something false, rejoice with me, because I too hear false things from antichrists. But if you heard something true, look to your conscience, and, if you are afraid of hearing something, be more afraid of being it."

11. *What you heard from the beginning, then, should abide in you. If what you heard from the beginning abides in you, you also will abide in the Son and the Father. This is the promise that he himself made to us.* (2:24-25) Perhaps you were looking for a reward, and you said, "See,

18. See Dn 3:24-90.
19. "Done ... made": *fecisti ... fecit.*
20. The reference to the chaff and the wind recalls the image of the winnowing on the Lord's threshing floor that appears in 5 above. See Mt 3:12.

what I heard from the beginning I am keeping and observing in myself. I am putting up with dangers, toil and trials for the sake of remaining in it. With what fruit? With what reward? What will he give me afterwards, since in this world I see myself toiling in the midst of trials? I see no rest at all here. Mortality itself weighs down my soul,[21] and my body, which is in the process of decay, presses it on to lower things. But I bear everything, so that what I heard from the beginning may abide in me. And I shall tell my God, *On account of the words from your lips I have kept hard ways* (Ps 16:4). With what reward?"

Listen and don't give up. If you were giving up in your toil, be strong for the sake of the promised reward. Who is it that works in a vineyard and lets it escape his heart what he is going to receive? Suppose that he has forgotten his reward and his hands droop. The recollection of the promised reward makes him persist in his work, and it was a human being who promised this, who is capable of failing you. How much stronger must you be in God's field, when Truth has made the promise, whose place no one can take, who cannot die, who cannot fail the one to whom he made his promise! And what is the promise? Let us see what he promised. Is it gold, which people greatly love here, or silver? Or possessions, for which people spend their gold, although they greatly love gold? Or pleasant estates, large houses, many slaves, numerous animals? This isn't the kind of reward that he is exhorting us to toil persistently for. What is this reward called? Eternal life. You heard, and you shouted joyfully.[22] Love what you have heard, and be freed from your toil for the sake of the rest of eternal life. See what God promises: eternal life. See what God threatens: eternal fire. What will he say to those who are placed on his right? *Come, blessed of my Father, receive the kingdom prepared for you from the origin of the world* (Mt 25:34). And to those on his left? *Go into the eternal fire that was prepared for the*

---

21. See Ws 9:15.
22. Here Augustine's congregation has reacted audibly to his words. See also VII,10. For congregational applause in Hippo see F. Van der Meer, *Augustine the Bishop: Church and Society at the Dawn of the Middle Ages*, trans. by B. Battershaw and G. R. Lamb (New York: Harper and Row, 1965) 427-432.

devil and his angels (Mt 25:41). If you don't love the former, at least fear the latter.

12. Remember, then, my brothers, that Christ has promised us eternal life. *This,* [John] says, *is the promise that he himself made to us, eternal life. I have written these things to you about those who are leading you astray.* (2:26) Let no one lead you astray to death. Long for the promise of eternal life. What can the world promise? Whatever it may promise, it promises to someone who will perhaps die tomorrow. And with what shame will you go out to him who abides forever? Suppose that a powerful man urges me with threats to do something bad. What does he threaten? Prison, chains, fire, torture, beasts? Eternal fire? Shudder at what the Almighty threatens, love what the Almighty promises, and the whole world becomes worthless, whether it promises or menaces.

I have written this to you about those who are leading you astray, so that you may know that you have an anointing,[23] *and so that the anointing which we have received from him may abide in us* (2:27). This is the sacrament of anointing, its invisible power itself being the invisible anointing that is the Holy Spirit.[24] The unseen anointing is that charity which, in whomever it is, will be like a root to him, and, despite the burning sun, it cannot dry up. Everything that is rooted is nourished by the sun's heat, and it doesn't dry up.

13. *And you do not need anyone to teach you, because his anointing teaches you about everything* (2:27). What are we doing, then, brothers, by teaching you? If his anointing teaches us about everything, it seems as though we are toiling to no avail. And to what purpose do we cry out so much? Let us leave you to his anointing, and his anointing will teach you. But now I ask myself and I ask the apostle himself a question. May he deign to hear the little one who is asking him. I say to John, "Did those to whom you were speaking have the anointing?" You said, *Because his anointing teaches you about everything*. Why did you write such an

---

23. This phrase is not in the Greek text of the epistle but must have been in the Latin text that Augustine was following.

24. Augustine seems to be alluding to the baptismal anointing, which followed the water baptism itself and was understood to confer the Holy Spirit. Here he emphasizes its invisible effects. See also 5 above and note 12.

epistle? What were you teaching them? What were you instructing them in? What were you building up?

Now see a great sacrament here, brothers: the sound of our words strikes the ears; the teacher is within. Don't think that a person learns anything from a human being.[25] We can offer a suggestion by the sound of our voice, but if he who teaches isn't within, our voice is of no avail. Well, brothers, do you want to know more? Haven't all of you heard this sermon? How many will leave from here untaught? As far as my role is concerned, I have spoken to everyone. But those to whom that unction doesn't speak within, whom the Holy Spirit doesn't teach within, depart untaught. Teachings and admonitions that come from without are of some help. He who teaches hearts has his chair in heaven. Hence even he himself says in the gospel, *Do not call anyone on earth your teacher; one is your teacher, the Christ* (Mt 23:8-9). Let him, then, speak to you within, when there are no human beings there, because, even if there is someone at your side, there is no one in your heart. And there should be no one in your heart; Christ should be in your heart; his anointing should be in your heart, so that your heart may not be thirsting in solitude, because it doesn't have the springs by which it may be refreshed. He who teaches, then, is the inner teacher: Christ teaches; his inbreathing teaches. Where his inbreathing and his anointing don't exist, words sound without to no avail.

These words which we are speaking from without, brothers, are like a farmer in respect to a tree. He works from without; he employs water and careful cultivation. Whatever he may employ from without, does *he* form the fruit? Does *he* cover the bare branches with the shade of foliage? Does *he* do any such thing from within? Who does this, then? Listen to the farmer-Apostle, and see what we are, and listen to the inner teacher: *I planted, Apollo watered, but God gave the growth. Neither is he who plants anything, nor he who waters, but God, who gives the growth.* (1 Cor 3:6-7) This is what I tell you, then: whether by our speaking we plant or water, we aren't anything, but he who gives the growth, God—that is, his anointing, which teaches you about everything.

---

25. This and what follows is an example of what could be called Augustine's pastoral realism. See Van der Meer 449-452.

Fourth Homily

1. Brothers, you remember that yesterday's reading concluded with this—that *you do not need anyone to teach you, but his anointing teaches you about everything* (2:27). We explained this to you, as I am sure that you recall, by saying that, when we speak to your ears from without, it is as though we are laborers who are cultivating a tree from without, but we are unable to give the growth or to form the fruit.[1] Unless he speaks to you within—he who created and redeemed and called you, who dwells in you through faith and his Spirit—we shout out to no purpose. How is this evident? Because, although many hear, what is said isn't persuasive to everyone but only to those to whom God speaks within. But he speaks within to those who make room for him. Those who make room for God, however, don't make room for the devil. For the devil wants to dwell in the hearts of men and to speak there all the things that are conducive to leading us astray. But what does the Lord Jesus say? *The prince of this world has been sent without* (Jn 12:31). Where was he sent to? Beyond heaven and earth? Beyond the structure of this world? No: beyond the hearts of believers. Once the intruder has been sent without, the redeemer may dwell there, because the very one who has created has redeemed. And the devil now assails from without; he doesn't conquer the one who possesses what is within. He assails from without by introducing various temptations. But the one to whom God speaks within and who possesses the anointing of which you have heard doesn't consent.

2. And that same anointing, [John] says, *is true*—that is, the Spirit of the Lord himself, who teaches human beings, is incapable of lying. *And it does not lie. As he taught you, abide in it. And now, little children, remain in it, and when he has been manifested, let us have faith in his presence, so that we may not be confounded by him at his coming.* (2:27-28) You see, brothers, we believe in Jesus, whom we can't see. They proclaimed him who saw him, who touched him, who heard the word from his own lips, and, in order to persuade the human race of these things, they were

---

1. See III,13.

sent by him; they didn't dare go by themselves. And where were they
sent? You heard when the gospel was read: *Go, preach the gospel to the
whole creation that is under heaven* (Mk 16:15). The disciples, then,
were sent everywhere, with signs and wonders attesting to them so that
they would be believed, because they spoke of what they had seen. And
we believe in him whom we haven't seen, and we look forward to him
when he comes. Whoever look forward to him in faith will rejoice when
he comes; those who are without faith will be ashamed when that comes
which they don't see now. That shame won't last one day and disappear,
as people who are found out in some misdeed are accustomed to be
ashamed, and who are mocked by human beings. That shame will lead
them, ashamed, to the left, so that they may hear: *Go into the eternal fire
that was prepared for the devil and his angels* (Mt 25:41). Let us abide in
his words, therefore, lest we be ashamed when he comes. He himself says
in the gospel to those who had believed in him, *If you remain in my word,
you are truly my disciples* (Jn 8:31). And, as if they were saying, " To
what purpose?" he said, *And you shall know the truth, and the truth shall
set you free* (Jn 8:32). For now our salvation is a matter of hope, not yet of
reality,[2] for we don't yet hold what has been promised, but we hope for
what is to come. But he who promised is faithful; he doesn't deceive you.
Just don't let yourself grow weak, but look forward to the promise, for
truth is incapable of being deceptive. Don't let yourself be a liar by
saying one thing and doing another. You keep faith, and he keeps his
promise. But if you don't keep faith, you—not he who made the
promise—have cheated yourself.

3. *If you know that he is righteous, know that everyone who acts righteously has been born of him* (2:29). Now our righteousness comes from
faith. There is no perfect righteousness except in the angels—and hardly
in the angels, if they are compared with God. Nonetheless, however
perfect the righteousness of the souls and spirits is whom God created, it
exists in the angels, who are holy, righteous, good, not turned away by
any fall, unyielding to any pride, but ever abiding in the contemplation of

2. "Hope ... reality" : *spe ... re*. The *spes-res* contrast/word-play is very frequent in Augustine; see
also VIII,13.

the Word of God and possessing no other sweetness apart from him by whom they were created. In them there is perfect righteousness. In us, however, it comes into existence from faith according to the Spirit.

You heard when the psalm was read: *Begin to the Lord in confession* (Ps 147:7). It says, *Begin*. The beginning of our righteousness is the confession of sins. When you have begun not to defend your sin, then you have started to be righteous. But it will be perfected in you when doing nothing else delights you, when death is swallowed up in victory,[3] when no concupiscence titillates you, when there is no struggle with flesh and blood,[4] when there is a crown of victory and triumph over the enemy: then there will be perfect righteousness. At present we are still fighting. If we are fighting, we are in the stadium; we win and we are won against, but he who will conquer is awaited. He conquers, however, who, even when winning, presumes not on his own strength but on God, his encourager. The devil alone fights against us. We, if we are with God, conquer the devil, for, if you fight alone with the devil, you will be conquered. The enemy is skillful. How many palms of victory does he have? Consider whither he cast us down. So that we would be born as mortals, he first cast our own ancestors themselves out of paradise. What must be done, then, inasmuch as he is skillful? The Almighty must be invoked against the skillful devil. Let him dwell in you who can't be conquered, and you will safely conquer him who is accustomed to conquer. But whom? Those in whom God doesn't dwell. For, as you know, brothers, Adam, when he was in paradise, disdained God's commandment and lifted his neck, as though desiring to be in his own power and not wishing to be subject to God's will, and he fell from that immortality, from that beatitude. But a certain skillful man who was born mortal conquered the devil, although he was sitting in dung and rotten with worms. And Adam himself conquered, and he did so in Job, because Job was of his race. Therefore Adam, who was conquered in paradise, conquered in dung. When he was in paradise, he listened to the persuading of a woman whom the devil had sent him. But when he was in

---

3. See 1 Cor 15:54.
4. This is a rare instance of pairing flesh and blood in this context. Ordinarily Augustine characterizes the spiritual struggle as being simply with the flesh, not also with blood.

dung he said to Eve, *You have spoken like one of the foolish women* (Jb 2:10). In the former case he lent his ear, in the latter he gave a response; when he was in an optimistic mood he listened, when he was beaten he conquered. See, then, what follows in the epistle, brothers, because it informs us that we may indeed conquer the devil, but not on our own. *If you know that he is righteous*, he says, *know that everyone who acts righteously has been born of him*—of God, of Christ. And, by saying *has been born of him*, it is encouraging us. Because we have already been born of him, then, we are perfect.

4. Listen: *See the kind of love that the Father has given us, so that we are called and are sons* (3:1). As far as concerns those who are called something and aren't it, what use is the title to them when there is no reality? How many are called doctors who don't know how to heal! How many are called watchful who sleep the whole night! Thus, many are called Christians, and they aren't found to be so in reality, because they aren't what they are called—that is, in life, in behavior, in faith, in hope, in charity. But what have you heard here, brothers? *See the kind of love that the Father has given us, so that we are called and are sons. This is why the world has not known us, because it did not know him, and the world does not know us.* (3:1)[5] The whole Christian world and the whole wicked world, for there are wicked persons throughout the world and there are good persons throughout the world: they don't know them. What makes us think that they don't know them? They scoff at those who lead good lives. Listen and see, because perhaps they are also in your midst. Whichever of you already lives in a good manner, disdains worldly things, doesn't want to attend the spectacles, doesn't want to get drunk in the customary fashion or—what is more serious—make himself unclean,[6] excusing himself by the approach of the holy days:[7] he who doesn't want to do these things, how is he not scoffed at by those who *do* do them! Would he be scoffed at if he were recognized? But why isn't he recognized? The world doesn't recognize him. Who are the world?

---

5. *And the world does not know us* is not in the original Greek text but must have been in Augustine's Latin version of the text.

6. The uncleanness to which Augustine is referring is probably illicit sexual activity.

7. The holy days are almost certainly the days of Easter.

Those who dwell in the world; it is their house, so to speak, and they dwell in it. These things have already been said many times, and I don't dislike repeating them to you. When you hear "the world" being given a bad meaning, you ought to understand it only as the lovers of the world, because they dwell there through love, and they have deserved to have this title from the reason why they dwell there. The world hasn't known us because it hasn't known him. Even the Lord Jesus Christ himself walked among us, God was in flesh, he hid himself in weakness. And how was he unknown? Because he rebuked all the sins in people. It was by loving the pleasures of their sins that they didn't recognize God. By loving what their sickness attracted them to, they acted against their physician.

5. What about us, then? We have now been born from him, but because we are in hope [John] says, *Beloved, we are now God's children* (3:2). Already? What are we waiting for, then, if we are already God's children? *And*, he says, *what we shall be has not yet been manifested* (3:2). But what shall we be other than God's children? Listen to what follows: *We know that, when he appears, we shall be like him, because we shall see him as he is* (3:2). Let Your Charity understand. This is a great matter: *We know that, when he appears, we shall be like him, because we shall see him as he is.* Now pay attention to the word *is*. You know it as a word. What "is" is as a word, and not only as a word but really is, is something unchangeable. It abides forever, it cannot be changed, it is not subject to decay in any part. It neither advances, because it is perfect, nor falls back, because it is eternal. And what is it? *In the beginning was the Word, and the Word was with God, and the Word was God* (Jn 1:1). And what is it? *Although he was in the form of God, he did not think it robbery to be equal to God* (Phil 2:6). The wicked can't see Christ in this way, in the form of God, as the Word of God, as the Only-Begotten of the Father, as equal to the Father. But, as far as the Word's having become flesh is concerned, even the wicked can see that, because on the day of judgment even the wicked will see him, because he will come to judge just as he had come to *be* judged—a man in terms of form itself, but God. For *cursed is everyone who places his hope in a man* (Jer 17:5). As a man he came to be judged, as a man he will come to

judge. And if he isn't seen, what are we to make of what is written, *They shall look upon him whom they transfixed* (Zec 12:10; Jn 19:37)? For of the wicked it is said that they shall see and be confounded. How will the wicked not see when he places the ones on his right and the others on his left? To those placed on his right he will say, *Come, blessed of my Father, receive the kingdom* (Mt 25:34). To those placed on his left he will say, *Go into the eternal fire* (Mt 25:41). They shall see only the form of a slave; the form of God they shall not see. Why? Because they are wicked, and the Lord himself says, *Blessed are the clean of heart, for they shall see God* (Mt 5:8). We are going to see a certain vision, therefore, brothers, *which neither the eye has seen nor the ear heard, nor has it entered into the heart of man* (1 Cor 2:9)—a certain surpassing vision that excels all the earthly beauties of gold, of silver, of glades and fields, the beauty of sea and sky, the beauty of sun and moon, the beauty of the stars, the beauty of the angels, all things, because it is from this that all things are beautiful.

6. What, then, shall we be when we see this? What has been promised us? *We shall be like him, because we shall see him as he is.* The tongue has sounded how this could be; let the rest be thought through by the heart. For what did John say when compared with him who is, and what can be said by us human beings who are utterly unequal to his merits?

Let us return, then, to that anointing of his. Let us return to that anointing which teaches within what we are unable to speak, and, because now you are unable to see, let your task consist in desiring. The entire life of a good Christian is a holy desire. What you desire, however, you don't yet see. But by desiring you are made large enough, so that, when there comes what you should see, you may be filled. For, if you wish to fill a purse, and you know how big what will be given you is, you stretch the purse, whether it is made of cloth or leather or anything else. You know how much you are going to obtain, and you see that your purse is small; by stretching it you make it that much larger. This is how God stretches our desire through delay, stretches our soul through desire, and makes it large enough by stretching it. Let us desire, then, brothers, because we have to be filled. See how Paul stretches his purse, so that he may be able to receive what is going to come. As he says, *Not that I have already received or am already perfect. Brothers, I do not think that I have laid hold* (Phil 3:12-13). What are you doing in this life, then, if you haven't yet laid hold? *But there is one thing: I have forgotten what is behind, I have stretched out to what is ahead; in accord with the plan[8] I pursue the victory of my lofty calling* (Phil 3:13-14). He said that he stretched himself out, and he said that was pursuing something according to a plan. He considered himself too little to lay hold of what neither the eye has seen nor the ear heard, nor has it entered into the heart of man. This is our life—to be exercised through desire. But, to the degree that a holy desire exercises us, we have cut off our desires from love of the world. I have already said at one time or another, "Empty what must be filled." You must be filled with the good; pour out the bad. Consider that God wants to fill you with honey. If you are full of vinegar, where will you put the honey? What the vessel was carrying must be poured out; the vessel itself must be cleaned; it must be cleaned, even strenuously and by rubbing, so that it may become suitable for a particular thing. We may misname it;[9] we may name it gold or name it wine, whatever we name what cannot be named, whatever we want to name it, it is called God.[10] And when we name it God, what have we named? Are these two syllables[11] all that we are looking toward? Whatever we have been able to name it, then, is inferior. Let us stretch out to him so that, when he comes, he may fill us. *We shall be like him, because we shall see him as he is.*

7. *And everyone who has this hope in him* (3:3). You see that he has situated us in hope. You see how the apostle Paul agrees with his fellow apostle: *In hope we have been saved. But hope that is seen is not hope.*

---

8. *Stretched out … in accord with the plan: extentus … secundum intentionem.* Augustine's Latin text for this passage from Phil pairs the verb *extendo* and the noun *intentio*, which are related.

9. The Latin edition used for this translation reads *maledicamus*, which can be translated as either "we may curse" or "we may name badly" or "misname." The latter possibility seems much more likely. It is also possible that Augustine said *mel dicamus* ("we may name it honey"), which would be in keeping with the previous lines.

10. Augustine is suggesting that honey (if he originally said *mel dicamus*), gold and wine, consonant with the images that he has used of a purse (in which gold could be put) and a vessel (in which honey or wine could be poured), are very inadequate metaphors for God. Even the term "God" is inadequate to him.

11. The two-syllabled word in Latin is *Deus.*

For does someone hope for what he sees? For if we hope for what we do not see, we await it in patience. (Rom 8:24-25) Patience itself exercises our hope. You stand fast yourself, for he is steadfast, and persevere in your journey, so that you may arrive, because he won't depart from where you are going. *And everyone who has this hope in him makes himself pure just as he himself is pure* (3:3). See how he hasn't removed your free will. As he said, *he makes himself pure.* Who makes us pure if not God? But God doesn't make you pure if you are unwilling. Therefore, because you unite your will to God, you make yourself pure. You make yourself pure not of yourself but through him who came to dwell in you. Yet, because you do something there by your will, something has been bestowed upon you. But it has been bestowed upon you so that you may say, as in the psalm, *Be my helper; do not abandon me* (Ps 27:9). If you say, *Be my helper,* you are doing something. For, if you are doing nothing, how is he helping you?

8. *Everyone who commits sin also does wickedness* (3:4). Let no one say, "Sin is one thing and wickedness is another." Let no one say, "I'm a sinful man but I'm not wicked." *Everyone who commits sin also does wickedness; sin is wickedness* (3:4). What, then, are we to do about our sins and wickedness? Listen to what he says: *And you know that he has been manifested in order to take away sin, and there is no sin in him* (3:5). He in whom there is no sin came in order to take away sin. For, if there were sin in him, it would have to be taken away from him; he himself wouldn't take it away. *Everyone who abides in him does not sin* (3:6). To the degree that he remains in him, he doesn't sin. *Everyone who sins has not seen him, nor has he known him* (3:6). This isn't surprising. We haven't seen him but we are going to see him; we haven't known him but we are going to know him. We believe in him whom we haven't known. Or have we perhaps known him by faith and haven't yet known him by sight? But it is in faith that we have both seen and known him. For, if faith doesn't yet see, why are we called enlightened?[12] There is an enlightenment by faith, there is an enlightenment by sight. Now, as we journey

---

12. This is a baptismal reference: in Christian antiquity baptism was commonly spoken of as "enlightenment," and the baptized were "enlightened" (*illuminati*).

along, we walk by faith, not by sight.[13] Hence, also, our righteousness is by faith, not by sight. Our righteousness will be perfect when we see by sight. Let us not now abandon that righteousness which is by faith, because *the righteous person lives by faith* (Rom 1:17), as the Apostle says. *Everyone who abides in him does not sin,* while *everyone who sins has not seen him, nor has he known him.* He who sins doesn't believe this; but, if he believes it, he doesn't sin as far as his faith is concerned.

9. *Little children, let no one lead you astray. He who acts righteously is righteous just as he also is righteous.* (3:7) When we have heard that we are righteous, *just as he also is,* should we think that we are equal to God? You ought to know the meaning of *just as.*[14] For [John] said a while before, *He makes himself pure just as he himself is pure.* Now then, is our purity on a par with and equal to God's purity, and our righteousness to God's righteousness? Who would say this? But "just as" is not always accustomed to be said with a view to equality. For example, if someone saw this large basilica and should want to make a smaller one, although maintaining its proportions, and if, for example, it is twice as long as it is wide, he would also make its length twice as long as its width. In that way it seems that he would have made it "just as" the other. But, for example, if this one has a hundred cubits, that one would have thirty; and it is "as,"[15] and it is unequal. You see that "just as" does not always refer to parity and equality. For example, see what a difference there is between a person's face and his image in a mirror. There is the face in the image and the face in the body, the image in imitation and the body in reality. And what are we saying? For just as there are eyes here, so there are there; and just as there are ears here, so there are ears there. The thing is unequal, but "just as" is said in terms of likeness.

We ourselves, therefore, have the image of God, but not that which the Son has, who is equal to the Father. Yet, if we ourselves weren't just as he is in some small measure, we would say that in no respect were we like him. Therefore he makes us pure just as he himself is pure, but he is pure from eternity, while we are pure by faith. We are righteous just as he

---

13. See 2 Cor 5:7.
14. "Just as": *sicut.*
15. "As": *sic.*

himself is also righteous, but he is such in very unchangeable perpetuity, while we are righteous by believing in him whom we don't see, so that we may eventually see him. And, when our righteousness is perfect, when we have become equal to the angels, even then it won't be equal to him. How removed is it from him now, therefore, when it won't be on a par then!

10. *He who commits sin is of the devil, because the devil sins from the beginning* (3:8). You know that *of the devil* means "imitating the devil." For the devil has made no one, has begotten no one, has created no one. But whoever imitates the devil, as though having been born of him, becomes the devil's child by imitation, not, strictly speaking, by birth. How are you a child of Abraham? Did Abraham beget you? It is like the Jews, who were children of Abraham and didn't imitate Abraham's faith; they became the devil's children. They were born of Abraham's flesh and didn't imitate Abraham's faith. If, then, those who were born of him were disinherited because they didn't imitate him, you who haven't been born of him will be made his child, and you will be his child by imitating him. And, if you imitate the devil, because he is conspicuous for his pride and wickedness in the face of God, you will be the devil's child by imitating him—not because he has created you or begotten you.

11. *For this the Son of God was manifested* (3:8). Ah, brothers, all sinners have been born from the devil insofar as they are sinners. Adam was made by God, but when he gave in to the devil he was born from the devil, and he begot all such as he was. We have been born with concupiscence itself, and, before we add to our trespasses, we are born from that condemnation. For, if we are born with no sin, why is it that infants are rushed to baptism so that they may be absolved?[16] Pay heed, then, brothers, to two births—Adam and Christ. These are two men, but one of them is man-man,

---

16. This is an excellent example of the application of the so-called *lex orandi lex credendi* (originally phrased as *legem credendi statuit lex orandi*), meaning that the rule of prayer determines the rule of faith. Thus the ancient practice associated with the baptismal liturgy (i.e., liturgical prayer), of baptizing infants very soon after birth, implies (if it is not already explicitly stated, as it is here) the doctrine of original sin. The connection between the speedy baptism of newborns and the sin of Adam is discussed clearly and at length as early as the mid-third century in Cyprian, Letter 64,2-6, where Cyprian strongly advises against postponing baptism even for a week.

while the other of them is man-God.[17] Because of the man-man we are sinners; because of the man-God we are made righteous. The former birth cast us down to death; the latter birth raised us up to life. The former birth brings sin along with itself; the latter birth frees us from sin. It was for this reason that Christ the man came, to absolve the sins of men. *For this the Son of God was manifested, to dissolve the works of the devil* (3:8).

12. I commend the rest to Your Charity, lest I burden you. This is the very issue that we are making an effort to resolve, that we call ourselves sinners, for, if someone says that he is without sin, he is a liar. And in the epistle of John himself we find: *And if we say that we do not have sin, we are deceiving ourselves* (1:8). For you ought to remember the previous words: *If we say that we do not have sin, we are deceiving ourselves, and the truth is not in us* (1:8). And on the other hand you hear in the following words: *He who has been born from God does not sin. He who commits sin has not seen him, nor has he known him. Everyone who commits sin is of the devil.* (3:8-9) From God there is no sin. Yet he terrifies us. How have we been born from God, and how do we say that we are sinners? Should we say that we haven't been born of God? And what do those sacraments accomplish in infants? What did John say? *He who has been born from God does not sin.* Yet John himself says, *If we say that we do not have sin, we are deceiving ourselves, and the truth is not in us.* This is a great and difficult issue, and I would focus Your Charity on its resolution. Tomorrow, in the Lord's name, we shall discuss what he has bestowed from himself.

---

17. "Man-man": *homo homo*; "man-God": *homo Deus*.

Fifth Homily

1. Listen attentively, I beg you, because the matter that is being analyzed in your presence is no small thing, and I have no doubt that, as you were attentively present yesterday, you have come together with [even] greater attention today.

For this isn't an insignificant issue—how it is said in the epistle, *He who has been born from God does not sin* (3:9), and how it was said previously in the same epistle, *If we say that we do not have sin, we are deceiving ourselves, and the truth is not in us* (1:8). What is he to do who is squeezed in the middle by both phrases from the same epistle? If he confesses that he is a sinner, he fears that it will be said to him: "Therefore you have not been born from God, because it is written: *He who has been born from God does not sin.*" But, if he says that he is righteous and doesn't have sin, he is struck with a blow from the other side from the same epistle: *If we say that we do not have sin, we are deceiving ourselves, and the truth is not in us.* A person who has been placed in the middle, then, has no idea what to say or what to confess or what to declare. It is dangerous for him to declare that he is without sin, and it isn't only dangerous but even untrue. *We deceive ourselves, and the truth is not in us, if we say that we do not have sin.*[1] But would that you didn't have it and could say it! For you would be speaking the truth, and in expressing the truth you wouldn't fear even the slightest trace of wickedness. But you are doing evil if you say this, because you are telling a lie. *The truth is not in us*, he says, *if we say that we do not have sin.* [John] doesn't say, "We did not have," lest perchance he seem to have spoken about past life. For that man[2] had sins, but he didn't begin to have them from God, from whom he was born. If it were thus, this question wouldn't be weighing on us, for we would say, "We used to be sinners, but now we have been made righteous; we used to have sin, but now we

---

1. Augustine inverts the word order of the phrase both here and in its next citation for greater effect.
2. "That man" (*homo iste*) is Adam.

75

don't have it." This isn't what he says, but what does he say? *If we say that we do not have sin, we are deceiving ourselves, and the truth is not in us.* On the other hand he says elsewhere, *He who has been born from God does not sin.* Wasn't John himself born from God? If John himself, who you have heard reclined on the Lord's breast,[3] wasn't born from God, would anyone dare to promise himself a rebirth that would take place in himself, which he who merited to recline on the Lord's breast didn't merit to have? Was he whom the Lord loved more than the others[4] the only one that he didn't beget from the Spirit?

2. Pay heed now to these words. I continue to remind you of our difficult straits so that, by your attentiveness, which is a prayer both for us and for you, God may clear our path and offer us a way out; thus no one will find in his word an occasion for his own perdition, since his word has been preached and put into writing exclusively for our healing and salvation. *Everyone who commits sin also does wickedness* (3:4). In case you make a distinction, *sin is wickedness* (3:4). In case you say, "I'm a sinner but I'm not wicked," *sin is wickedness. And you know that he has been manifested in order to take away sin, and there is no sin in him.* (3:5) And what good is it to us that he came without sin? *Everyone who does not sin abides in him, and everyone who sins has not seen him, nor has he known him. Little children, let no one lead you astray. He who acts righteously is righteous just as he also is righteous.* (3:6-7) We have already said that "just as" is usually said in terms of a certain likeness, not in terms of equality.[5] *He who commits sin is of the devil, because the devil sins from the beginning* (3:8). And we said this because the devil created no one, nor did he beget anyone. But his imitators are as though born from him. *For this the Son of God was manifested, to dissolve the works of the devil* (3:8). He who doesn't have sin came,[6] then, to absolve sins.

Then there follows: *Everyone who has been born from God does not commit sin, because his seed abides in him, and he cannot sin, because*

---

3. See Jn 13:23.
4. See ibid.
5. See IV,9.
6. "Came" (*venit*) is missing from the manuscripts but has been supplied by the editors of the Latin text.

he has been born from God (3:9). He has backed us into a corner! Perhaps it was in terms of a particular sin that he said, *He does not sin*, rather than in terms of every sin. Thus, when he says, *He who has been born from God does not sin*, you should understand a particular sin which a person who has been born from God cannot commit, and it is the sort of sin that, if anyone committed it, would confirm the others, whereas, if someone didn't commit it, it would absolve the others. What is this sin? To act against the commandment. What is the commandment? *A new commandment I give you, that you love one another* (Jn 13:34). Pay attention. This commandment of Christ is called love. By this love sins are absolved. If this isn't maintained, it is both a grave sin and the root of all sins.

3. Pay attention, brothers. We have produced something in which the issue is resolved for those who think clearly. But are we only walking along this path with those who are quicker? Those who walk more slowly mustn't be left behind. Let us discuss this with the words that are at our disposal, so that it may be accessible to all.

For I think, brothers, that every person—who doesn't enter the Church without reason, who doesn't look for temporal goods in the Church, who doesn't enter in order to engage in worldly business but enters in order to grasp the eternal promise for himself, so that he may arrive at it—is concerned for his own soul. He must reflect on how to walk on the way, lest he stay behind, lest he go back, lest he wander off, lest he fail to arrive by going haltingly. He who is concerned, then, be he slow or fast, mustn't depart from the way. I have said this, then, because perhaps he wished *he who has been born from God does not sin* to be understood in terms of a particular sin, for it will be contrary to the former passage: *If we say that we do not have sin, we are deceiving ourselves, and the truth is not in us.* This, then, is how the issue can be resolved. There is a particular sin that he who has been born from God cannot commit, and by its not having been committed the others are absolved, and by its having been committed the others are confirmed.

What is this sin? To act against Christ's commandment, against the New Testament. What is the new commandment? *A new commandment I give you, that you love one another.* He who acts against charity and against brotherly love shouldn't dare to boast and to say that he has been born from God. But, as for him who is established in brotherly love, there are certain sins that he cannot commit, and in particular this one—that he hate his brother. And what is there to do about the other sins, of which it is said, *If we say that we do not have sin, we are deceiving ourselves, and the truth is not in us*? Listen to the security that comes from another passage of scripture: *Charity covers a multitude of sins* (1 Pt 4:8).

4. Therefore I commend charity. This epistle commends charity. After his resurrection what else did the Lord ask Peter than *Do you love me?* (Jn 21:15) It wasn't enough to ask once; again he asked nothing else, and a third time nothing else. At the third time, however, Peter, as though unaware of what the matter was, was upset by the Lord's apparent disbelief. Yet he asked this a first time, a second time and a third time. Three times fear denied,[7] three times love confessed.[8] See, Peter loves the Lord. What is he going to offer the Lord? For it isn't the case that in the psalm even [the psalmist] himself was untroubled: *What shall I give to the Lord for all that he has given to me?* (Ps 116:12) For he who said this in the psalm was conscious of how much had been offered him by God, and he looked for something to give to God and didn't find it. For whatever you wish to give to him you have received from him for the purpose of giving it back. And what did he find to give? As we said, brothers—what he had received from him, this he found to give. *I shall take the cup of salvation and shall invoke the name of the Lord* (Ps 116:13). For who had given him the saving cup but him to whom he wanted to give? To receive the saving cup, however, and to invoke the name of the Lord is to be filled with charity, and to be filled with charity in such a way that you not only don't hate your brother but are prepared to die for your brother. The Lord himself manifested this in himself when, as he was dying for all, he prayed for those by whom he was being crucified, and said, *Father, forgive them, for they do not know what they are doing* (Lk 23:34). But, if he was the only one to do this and he had no disciples, he was no teacher.

---

7. See Jn 18:17-27.
8. See Jn 21:15-17.

The disciples who followed him did this. Stephen was being stoned, and as he knelt down he said, *Lord, do not hold this crime against them* (Acts 7:60). He loved those by whom he was being killed, since he also died for them. Listen as well to the apostle Paul: *And I myself am being expended for the sake of your souls* (2 Cor 12:15). Now he was among those for whom Stephen prayed when he was dying at their hands.[9]

This, then, is perfect charity. If anyone has such charity that he is even prepared to die for his brothers, in him there is perfect charity. But as soon as it is born, is it already nearly perfect? It is born in order to be perfected; when it is has been born it is nursed; when it has been nursed it is fortified; when it has been fortified it is perfected. When it has come to perfection, what is there to say? *For me to live is Christ, and to die is gain. I wished to be dissolved and to be with Christ, for this was by far the best thing; to remain in the flesh is necessary for your sake.* (Phil 1:21-24) He wanted to live for the sake of those for whom he was prepared to die.

5. And, so that you may know that perfect charity is that which he who has been born from God doesn't violate and against which he doesn't sin, this is what the Lord says to Peter: *Peter, do you love me?* And he says, *I love you.* (Jn 21:17) He didn't say, "If you love me, be kind to me." For, when the Lord was in mortal flesh, he hungered, he thirsted. At the time when he hungered and thirsted, he was received as a guest. Those who had possessions ministered to him from their substance, as we read in the gospel. Zacchaeus received him as a guest: he was cured of a disease when he received his physician as his guest. Of what disease? Avarice. For he was very rich, and the chief of the tax collectors. Listen to how he was cured of the disease of avarice: *I give half of my possessions to the poor, and, if I have taken anything from anyone, I will return it fourfold* (Lk 19:8). Hence he saved the other half not to enjoy but to pay off his debts.

He received his physician as a guest at that time, then, because in the Lord there was fleshly frailty to which people might offer this kindness. And this was the case because he wanted to offer something to those who

---

9. See Acts 7:58.

were kind to him, for it benefited those who were offering the kindness and not him. For what kindness of theirs was he, to whom angels used to minister, looking for? His servant Elijah, for whom he provided bread and meat by way of a raven, never had this need, and yet, so that a devout widow would be blessed, the servant of God is sent and is fed by the widow, whom God was secretly feeding.[10] But, although by means of these servants of God those who reflect on their poverty make an offering to themselves, it is for the sake of that reward from the Lord, which is very clearly mentioned in the gospel: *He who receives a righteous person under the title of a righteous person shall receive a righteous person's reward, and he who receives a prophet under the title of a prophet shall receive a prophet's reward, and he who gives a cup of cold water to one of these least ones simply under the title of a disciple—amen I say to you—shall not lose his reward* (Mt 10:41-42). Although, therefore, those who do this make an offering to themselves, yet he was unable to have this offered to him once he had ascended into heaven. What was Peter, who loved him, able to give him? Listen to what it was: *Feed my sheep* (Jn 21:15)—that is, "Do for the brothers what I have done for you. I have redeemed all with my own blood. Don't hesitate to die for confessing the truth, so that others may imitate you."

6. Now this, as we have said, brothers, is perfect charity. He who has been born from God possesses it. Let Your Charity pay heed; see what I shall say.

See, a baptized person has received the sacrament of birth. He has the sacrament, and it is a great, divine, holy and ineffable sacrament. Consider what sort of thing it is—that it makes a person new by the forgiveness of all his sins. Yet let him look into his own heart [to see] if what happened in his body was perfected there.[11] Let him see if he has charity, and then let him say, "I have been born from God." But, [even] if

---

10. See 1 K 17:4-9.
11. What happened in a person's body in a typical baptism was an immersion in water and at least one anointing with oil.

he doesn't have it, he does indeed have a mark placed on him,[12] but he is a deserter on the run. Let him have charity; otherwise let him not say that he has been born from God. "But," he says, "I have the sacrament." Listen to the Apostle: *If I know all sacraments*[13] *and have all faith, such that I may move mountains, but do not have charity, I am nothing* (1 Cor 13:2).

7. We commended this, if you remember, when we began to read this epistle: there is nothing in it that is as much commended to us as charity. And, if [John] seems to say other things from time to time, that is where he returns, and whatever he says he wants to apply to that charity. Let us see if he does this here as well. Pay attention: *Everyone who has been born from God does not commit sin.* We are looking for the meaning of *sin*, because, if we understand it to refer to every kind, it will be contrary to the passage: *If we say that we do not have sin, we are deceiving ourselves, and the truth is not in us.* Let him say what sin is, therefore; let him teach us, in case I rashly said that this sin was a violation of charity, because he said previously, *He who hates his brother is in darkness, and he walks in darkness and does not know where he is going, because the darkness has blinded his eyes* (2:11). But perhaps he said something in later passages and mentioned charity.[14] See that this roundabout way with words has this goal, has this aim. *Everyone who has been born from God does not sin, because his seed abides in him.* The seed of God is the word of God, which is why the Apostle says, *I have begotten you through the gospel* (1 Cor 4:15). *And he cannot sin, because he has been born from God.* Let him say this, let us see how he cannot sin. *This is how the children of God and the children of the devil are manifested: everyone who is not righteous and who does not love his brother is not of God.* (3:10) Surely there is now manifested why he said, *And who*, he says, *does not love his brother.* •

---

12. The "mark" (*character*) is a quality that cannot be destroyed and that brands the baptized person forever, whether he be good or bad. On Augustine's sizable contribution to the theology of sacramental character, which continues to influence the Western understanding of the sacraments, see *Dictionnaire de Théologie Catholique* II/2.1699-1701.

13. "Sacraments" (*sacramenta*) is here interchangeable with the more familiar "mysteries."

14. An alternative reading adds a *non*: "But perhaps he said something in later passages and did *not* mention charity."

Love alone, then, distinguishes between the children of God and the children of the devil. All may sign themselves with the sign of Christ's cross; all may respond "Amen"; all may sing "Alleluia"; all may be baptized; all may go into the churches; all may construct the walls of basilicas.[15] The children of God aren't distinguished from the children of the devil except by charity. Those who have charity have been born from God; those who don't have it haven't been born from God. This is a great indication, a great distinction. Have whatever you will, [but] if you don't have this alone, nothing is of benefit to you. If you have nothing else, have this and you have fulfilled the law. *For he who loves his neighbor has fulfilled the law* (Rom 13:8), says the Apostle. And *charity is the fulfillment of the law* (Rom 13:10).

I think that this is the pearl which the merchant is described as having found in the gospel, who found one pearl and sold everything that he had and purchased it.[16] This is the costly pearl, charity, without which nothing whatsoever that you may have is of any benefit to you, but which, if you have it alone, is enough for you. You see now with faith; then you will see by appearance. For, if we love when we don't see, how we shall embrace when we do see! But where must we practice? In brotherly love. You can tell me, "I haven't seen God." Can you tell me, "I haven't seen a human being"? Love your brother. For, if you love the brother whom you see, you will see God at the same time, because you will see charity itself, and God dwells within it.

8. *Everyone who is not righteous and who does not love his brother is not from God. For this is the message.* (3:11) See how [John] confirms it: *For this is the message that we have heard from the beginning, that we should love one another* (3:11). He made clear to us that he spoke with this in mind: whoever acts against this commandment is in that vicious sin which those who aren't born from God fall into. *Not like Cain, who was from the evil one, and he killed his brother. And why did he kill him? Because his deeds were evil, whereas his brother's were righteous.*

---

15. Although Rettig translates these words similarly, he suggests that Burnaby's rendering—"line the walls of the basilica"—may make sense; i.e., people who throng to the basilicas press against their walls.

16. See Mt 13:46.

(3:12) Where envy exists, then, there can be no brotherly love. Let Your Charity be attentive. He who is envious doesn't love. The devil's sin is in him, because the devil himself cast man down through envy. For he fell, and he was envious of someone who was standing. He didn't want to cast him down so that he himself might stand but so that he wouldn't be the only one to fall. Keep in mind from this what he added, that there cannot be envy in charity. This should be evident to you from when that very charity was being praised: *Charity is not envious* (1 Cor 13:4). There was no charity in Cain, and, if there had been no charity in Abel, God wouldn't have accepted his sacrifice. For, when they both made their offering, the one of the fruits of the earth, the other of lambs, what do you think, brothers—that God ignored the fruits of the earth and loved the lambs?[17] God didn't regard the hands but looked in the heart, and he had regard for the sacrifice of him whom he saw offering it with charity; he averted his eyes from the sacrifice of him whom he saw offering it with envy. He calls Abel's good deeds nothing other than charity; he calls Cain's evil deeds nothing other than brotherly hatred. It isn't enough that he hated his brother and envied his good deeds; because he didn't want to imitate him, he wanted to kill him. And from this it was clear that he was a son of the devil, and from this it was clear that the other was a righteous man of God. It is on this basis, then, my brothers, that people are distinguished. Let no one pay attention to words but to actions and to the heart. If a person doesn't act rightly with respect to his brothers, he shows what he has in himself. People are proved by their temptations.

9. *Do not be surprised, brothers, if the world hates us* (3:13). Must you be told frequently what the world is? Neither heaven, nor earth, nor the works that God has made, but the lovers of the world.[18] Because I often speak of these things I am tedious to some people. But to such a degree is what I say not pointless that some were asked whether I spoke, and they

---

17. See Gn 4:1-8.
18. See also IV,4.

would not respond.[19] Indeed, by pressing the issue, then, something may stick in the hearts of my listeners.

What is the world? When it is understood in a bad sense, it is the lovers of the world. When it is understood in a praiseworthy sense, it is heaven and earth and the works of God that are in them. Hence it is said, *And the world was made through him* (Jn 1:10). Likewise, the world is the fullness of the earth, as John himself said, *He is the propitiator not only for our sins but also for those of the whole world* (2:2). *World* refers to all believers scattered throughout the earth. But in a bad sense the world is the lovers of the world. Those who love the world cannot love their brother.

10. *If the world hates us, we know* (3:14). What do we know? *That we have passed from death to life* (3:14). How do we know it? *Because we love the brothers* (3:14). Let no one question anyone. Let each person return to his own heart; if he finds brotherly charity there, he should be secure, because he has passed from death to life. He is already on the right side.[20] He shouldn't be concerned that his glory is presently hidden; when the Lord comes, then he will appear in glory. For he is alive, but he is in winter. The root is alive, but the branches are as though dry. Within is the vital core that gives life, within are the leaves, within is the fruit, but they are waiting for summer. Therefore *we know that we have passed from death to life because we love the brothers. He who does not love remains in death* (3:15). Lest you think, brothers, that it is something trivial to hate or not to love, listen to what follows: *Everyone who hates his brother is a murderer* (3:15). If, then, someone considered brotherly hatred insignificant, is he also going to consider murder insignificant in his heart?[21] His hand doesn't move to kill a man, but he is already seen as a murderer by the Lord. One is alive, and another is already judged as his killer. *Everyone who hates his brother is a murderer, and you know that no murderer has eternal life abiding in him* (3:15).

---

19. Augustine seems to be saying that some people were paying so little attention to him that they couldn't even remember whether he had actually spoken.
20. See Mt 25:33-34.
21. This phrase may also be reasonably translated: "is he also going to consider the murder in his heart insignificant?"

11. *This is how we know love* (3:16). He is referring to the perfection of love—the perfection that we have spoken of. *This is how we know love, that he has laid down his life for us, and we must lay down our lives for our brothers* (3:16). See where this came from: *Peter, do you love me? Feed my sheep.* So that you would know that this was how he wanted his sheep to be fed by him, by laying down his life for his sheep, he immediately added this: *When you were young, you used to gird yourself, and you used to go where you wanted; but now that you are older, someone else shall gird you and shall take you where you do not want to go. He said this,* the evangelist said, *in order to signify by what death he was going to glorify God.* (Jn 21:18-19) It was thus that he taught him to whom he had said, *Feed my sheep,* to lay down his life for his sheep.

12. How does charity begin, brothers? Pay attention briefly. You have heard how charity is perfected.[22] In the gospel the Lord noted its very goal and manner: *Greater charity no one has,* he says, *than to lay down his life for his friends* (Jn 15:13). He showed you its perfection in the gospel, then, and here its perfection was noted, but you ask yourselves and say to yourselves, "When can we have this charity?" Don't be quick to lose hope for yourself: it was born strong but isn't yet perfect; nurse it so that it won't be smothered. But you will say to me, "How do I know this?" We have heard how it is perfected; let us listen to how it begins.

In what follows he says, *But he who had the goods of the world and saw his brother hungry and closed his heart to him—how will God's love be able to abide in him?* (3:17) Look, this is where charity begins. If you aren't yet ready to die for your brother, be ready to give of your goods to your brother. Let charity strike your heart now, so that you don't act for the sake of display but out of mercy's inmost marrow, so that you consider him as one who is suffering want. For, if you can't give what is superfluous to your brother, how can you lay down your life for your brother? There is money in your purse that thieves could take from you, and, if thieves didn't take it, you might lose it by dying, even if it hadn't left you during your lifetime. What will you do with it then? Your brother

---

22. The contrast with charity's beginning would be more evident if "perfected" (*perficiatur*) were rendered instead as "completed." But charity as perfectible is overall a richer concept than charity as complete-able.

is hungry, he is needy. Perhaps he is anxious[23] and is being pressed by a creditor. He has nothing, you have something. He is your brother. You have been purchased together; your price is the same;[24] both of you have been redeemed by the blood of Christ. See if you are merciful, if you have the goods of the world. Perhaps you are saying, "What does this have to do with me? Am I going to give away my money so that he won't be troubled?" If this is how your heart responds to you, the Father's love doesn't abide in you. If the Father's love doesn't abide in you, you haven't been born from God. How do you boast of being a Christian? You have the name and you don't have the deeds. But, should someone call you a pagan, if action comes with the name, show that you are a Christian by your deeds. For, if you don't show yourself a Christian by your deeds, everyone may call you a Christian, but what good is the name where there is no reality? *But he who had the goods of the world and saw his brother hungry and closed his heart to him—how will God's love be able to abide in him?* And there follows: *Little children, let us not love only in word and speech but in action and truth* (3:18).

13. I think that the great and indispensable mystery and sacrament has been manifested to you, my brothers. All of scripture commends charity's worth, but I don't know if it is commended anywhere more expansively than in this epistle. I ask and beseech you in the Lord both to remember what you have heard and to come attentively and to listen attentively to those things that must still be said, until this epistle is finished. Open your heart to the good seeds; get rid of the thorns, lest what is being sown in you be smothered; instead, let the crop grow! That is how the farmer may rejoice and how you may prepare for yourself, so to speak, a storehouse for grain and not a fire for chaff.[25]

---

23. "Anxious": *suspenditur*, i.e., in a state of suspense. But it could also be that the person in question has been hung or suspended at a whipping post until he has paid his debt.
24. See 1 Cor 6:20; 7:23.
25. See Mt 3:12; 13:30.

Sixth Homily

1. If you remember, brothers, we concluded our sermon yesterday with this phrase, which certainly should have remained and ought to abide in your heart, because you heard it at the very end: *Little children, let us not love only in word and speech but in action and truth* (3:18). Then there follows: *And this is how we know that we are of the truth and assure our heart in his presence—that, if our heart thinks badly, God is greater than our heart, and he knows all things* (3:19-20). [John] had said, *Let us not love only in word and speech but in action and truth.* It is asked of us by what action and by what truth he who loves God, or he who loves his brother, is recognizable. He had already said previously to what point charity might be perfected, which the Lord also says in the gospel: *Greater charity no one has than to lay down his life for his friends* (Jn 15:13). And John had said this: *Just as he laid down his life for us, we also must lay down our lives for our brothers* (3:16). This is the perfection of charity, and greater can never be found.

But, because it isn't perfect in everyone, he in whom it isn't perfect shouldn't lose hope, if what has already been born is what must be perfected; and, indeed, if it has been born, it must be nursed and must be brought by those who are nursing it to its proper perfection. We have been looking for the inception of charity and where it begins, and immediately following we find there: *If someone has the goods of the world and sees his brother needy and closes his heart against him—how does the Father's love abide in him?* (3:17) It is here, then, that this charity begins, brothers, when one bestows one's superfluities on a needy person who is in difficult circumstances and when, from what he possesses in abundance in a temporal way, he frees his brother from temporal tribulation. Here is the commencement of charity. If you nurse this beginning by the word of God and the hope of future life, that is how you will arrive at that perfection, with the result that you will be ready to lay down your life for your brothers.

2. But, because many such things are done by those who are in pursuit of other things and who don't love their brothers, let us return to the testimony of conscience. How do we prove that many such things are done by those who don't love their brothers? How many there are who are involved in heresies and schisms and who call themselves martyrs! They seem to themselves to be laying down their life for their brothers. If they were laying down their life for their brothers, they wouldn't be separating themselves from the whole brotherhood. Likewise, how many there are who give away much and who donate much for the sake of display, and who are looking for nothing but human praise and the people's acclaim, which is full of wind and utterly fickle! Because there are such people, then, where will brotherly charity be proved? Because he wanted it to be proved and said in a tone of warning, *Little children, let us not love only in word and speech but in action and truth.* We ask in what action and in what truth. Can an action be more overt than giving to the poor? There are many who do this for the sake of display, not out of love. Can an action be greater than dying for one's brothers? And there are many who want it to be thought that they are doing this, who must be judged by the display of their name and not by their loving heart. The upshot is that he loves his brother who, before God, where he alone sees, assures his heart and questions his heart as to whether he is really doing this on account of brotherly love, and the eye that penetrates the heart, where a human being cannot gaze, testifies to him. The apostle Paul was ready to die for his brothers, and he said, *I myself am being expended for the sake of your souls* (2 Cor 12:15). Yet, because God saw this in his heart, not the human beings to whom he was speaking, he said to them, *But to me it is very little that I should be judged by you or by man's day* (1 Cor 4:3). And he himself also shows in a particular passage that these things are often done for vain display, not on the firm basis of charity, inasmuch as, when he was commending this very charity, he said, *If I distribute everything that I have to the poor and hand over my body to be burned but do not have charity, it is of no benefit to me* (1 Cor 13:3). Can someone do this without charity? He can. For those who don't have charity have brought division to unity. Look around and you will see

many persons giving much to the poor; you will see others so ready to embrace death that, after the persecutor has stopped, they throw themselves on him.[1] There is no doubt that they are doing this without charity.

Let us return, then, to our conscience, of which the Apostle says, *For this is our glory, the testimony of our conscience* (2 Cor 1:12). Let us return to our conscience, of which he says again, *But let each person prove his own work, and then he will have glory in himself and not in another* (Gal 6:4). Let each of us, then, prove his own work—whether it emanates from an innate charity, whether the branches of good works spring from the root of love. *But let each person prove his own work*, he says, *and then he will have glory in himself and not in another*—not when someone else's tongue bears witness to him but when his own conscience bears it.

3. This is what [John] commends here, then. *This is how we know that we are of the truth*, when we love in action and truth, not only in words and speech, *and assure our heart in his presence*. What does *in his presence* mean? Where he himself sees. Hence, the Lord himself says in the gospel, *Beware of practicing your righteousness in the presence of men, in order to be seen by them; otherwise you will not have a reward with your Father who is in heaven* (Mt 6:1). And what does this mean—*Your left hand should not know what your right hand is doing* (Mt 6:3)—if not that the right hand is a pure conscience while the left hand is the world's desire?[2] There are many who through the world's desire perform many marvels; it is the left hand, not the right, that accomplishes them. The right hand must accomplish them unbeknownst to the left hand, so that the world's desire may not intrude when we are accomplishing something good out of love. And where do we see this? You are before God. Question your heart: see what you have done and what you have been yearning for there—your salvation or the windy praise of men. Look within, for a person cannot judge one whom he cannot see. If we are assuring our heart, let us assure it in his presence.

---

1. The Donatists, of whom Augustine is speaking here, embraced a cult of persecution and martyrdom.
2. The symbolism of the right as good and the left as evil is exceedingly ancient in origin. It appears in the New Testament most notably in Mt 25:31-46.

Because if our heart thinks badly—that is, if it accuses us within, because we aren't acting with the spirit with which we should be acting —*God is greater than our heart, and he knows all things.* You hide your heart from man; hide it from God if you can. How will you hide it from him to whom it was said by a certain sinner in fear and confession: *Where shall I go from your spirit, and where shall I flee from your face?* (Ps 139:7) He was asking where he might flee in order to avoid God's judgment, and he found nowhere. For where does God not exist? *If,* he said, *I go up to heaven, you are there; if I go down to hell, you are present* (Ps 139:8). Where will you go? Where will you flee? Do you want to hear some advice? If you want to flee *from* him, flee *to* him. Flee *to* him by confessing, not *from* him by hiding, for you cannot hide, but you can confess. Tell him, *You are my refuge* (Ps 32:7), and let there be nursed in you the love that alone leads to life. Let your conscience bear testimony to you, because it is from God.[3] If it is from God, don't desire to extol it before men, because the praises of men don't lift you up to heaven, nor do their curses cast you down from there. Let him who crowns you see it; let him be your witness by whom, as your judge, you are crowned. *God is greater than our heart, and he knows all things.*

4. *Beloved, if our heart does not think badly, we have confidence with respect to God* (3:22). What does it mean that *our heart does not think badly?* That it has replied to us with the truth—that we love, and that there is a genuine love[4] in us which isn't feigned but sincere, seeking our brother's salvation and expecting no advantage from our brother apart from his salvation. *We have confidence with respect to God, and whatever we ask for we shall receive from him, because we are keeping his commandments* (3:22). Not in the sight of men, therefore, but where God himself sees in the heart. *We have confidence,* then, *with respect to God, and whatever we ask for we shall receive from him*—but *because we are keeping his commandments.* What are his commandments? Must this

---

3. "Let your conscience bear testimony to you, because it is from God": *Perhibeat tibi testimonium conscientia tua, quia ex Deo est.* The subject of *perhibeat* may be either "the love that alone leads to life" or "your conscience." Browne and Rettig opt for the former.

4. "Genuine love": *germana dilectio.* See also, later in the section, "genuine root" (*germanam ... radicem*). Augustine's use of *germana* is perhaps purposely ambiguous, since it can also mean "fraternal."

always be repeated? *A new commandment I give you, that you love one another* (Jn 13:34). He is speaking of charity itself; he is commending it. Whoever has brotherly charity, then, and has it in God's presence, where God sees, and his heart, having been put to the question in a just interrogation, doesn't respond to him in any other way than that there is the genuine root of charity there, from which good fruits may come forth—he has confidence with God, and whatever he asks for he will receive from him, because he is keeping his commandments.

5. There is a particular question that arises, which isn't a matter of one person or another, or you or me, asking for something from the Lord our God and not receiving it. In such a case it can be easy for someone to say of me, "He doesn't have charity." This can easily be said of anyone of this day and age. Let anyone think what he wants of anyone else: they aren't raising a very important question.[5] It is a matter, instead, of those men who were clearly holy when they were writing and are now with God.[6] Who has charity if Paul didn't have it, who said, *Our mouth is open to you, O Corinthians; our heart has been enlarged; you are not made narrow in us* (2 Cor 6:11-12); who said, *I am being expended for the sake of your souls* (2 Cor 12:15); and there was such grace in him that it was obvious that he had charity? Yet we find that he asked and didn't receive. What is there to say, brothers? It is a question. Be intent upon God. This too is a great question. What about sin, where it is said, *He who has been born from God does not sin* (3:9)? We have found that this sin is the one that violates charity, and it was properly designated in this place. So now as well we ask what he was saying. For if you pay heed to the words, it seems clear; if to examples, it is obscure. As far as these words are concerned, nothing is clearer: *And whatever we ask for we shall receive from him, because we are keeping his commandments, and we are doing what is pleasing to him in his sight* (3:22). *Whatever we ask for*, he says, *we shall receive from him.*

[John] has created great difficulties. He would also have created difficulties there if he were speaking of every sin. But we have found room to

---

5. Here Augustine has switched from the third person singular (*sentiat*) to the third person plural (*faciunt*).
6. The entire section that concludes here is in particularly awkward Latin and strongly suggests that Augustine was speaking spontaneously. It is interesting that he uses as models of holiness only the authors of the New Testament, and, in the end, only Paul.

explain, inasmuch as he spoke of a certain sin, not of every one—but of a particular sin that no one who has been born from God commits; and we have found that that particular sin itself is a violation of charity. And we have a clear example from the gospel when the Lord says, *If I had not come, they would not have sin* (Jn 15:22). What then? Had he come to the innocent Jews, because he speaks that way? Hence, if he hadn't come, would they not have sin? Did the physician's presence create illness, then, and not remove the fever? Who would be so mad as to say this? He didn't come except to cure and heal the sick. Why, then, did he say, *If I had not come, they would not have sin*, if not because he wanted a certain particular sin to be understood? For the Jews wouldn't have a particular sin.[7] What sin? That whereby they didn't believe in him, that whereby they disdained him when he was present. Hence, just as he spoke of a sin there, and it does not follow that we should understand every sin but rather a certain sin, neither is he speaking here of every sin (lest this contradict that passage where he says, *If we say that we do not have sin, we are deceiving ourselves, and the truth is not in us* [1:8]) but rather of a certain particular sin—that is, the violation of charity. But here he has constrained us still more. If we ask, he says, if our heart doesn't accuse us, and it declares in the sight of God that there is true love in us, *whatever we ask for we shall receive from him*.

6. I have already said to Your Charity, brothers, that no one should look to us.[8] For what are we? Or what are you? What except the Church of God, which is known to all? And, if it pleases him, we are in it, and we who abide in it through love should persevere in it if we want to show the love that we have.

But what bad thing shall we think of the apostle Paul? Didn't he love his brothers? Didn't he have with him the testimony of his conscience in the sight of God? Wasn't there in Paul that root of charity from which all good fruits proceeded? Who is so mad as to have said this? Where, then, do we find that the Apostle asked and didn't receive? He himself says, *Lest I be boastful because of the greatness of my revelations, there was given me a*

---

7. I.e., if Christ hadn't come, the Jews wouldn't have been guilty of the particular sin of disbelief, as Augustine explains in the ensuing lines.

8. See the beginning of 5 above.

goad for my flesh, an angel of Satan, to punish me. On its account I beseeched the Lord three times to remove it from me, and he told me, My grace is enough for you, for strength is perfected in weakness. (2 Cor 12:7-9) See, his prayer that the angel of Satan be removed from him wasn't answered. But why? Because it wasn't beneficial for him. Hence, he whose prayer wasn't heard in accord with his wish was answered with a view to his salvation. Your Charity should know the great sacrament[9] that we commend to you, lest it slip away from you during your trials. The prayers of the saints are answered in every respect; they are always answered with a view to eternal salvation. This is what they themselves desire, and it is for that reason that they are always answered.

7. But let us distinguish the ways in which God answers prayers. For we have found that some are not answered in accord with a person's wish and that others are answered with a view to his salvation, and, on the other hand, we have found that some *are* answered in accord with a person's wish and that others are *not* answered with a view to his salvation. Make this distinction, hold onto the example of him who wasn't answered in accord with his wish but was answered with a view to his salvation. Listen to the apostle Paul, for God gave him an answer precisely with a view to his salvation. *"My grace is enough for you,* he says, *for strength is perfected in weakness.* You beseeched, you cried out, you cried out three times. The very thing that you cried out I heard the first time; I didn't turn my ears away from you. I know what I should do. You want to remove the medicine by which you are being burned; I know the weakness by which you are being weighed down." And so his prayer was answered with a view to his salvation, but it wasn't heard in accord with his wish.

Which prayers have we found were answered in accord with a person's will but weren't answered with a view to his salvation? Have we found, do we think, some wicked person, some bad person, whose prayer was answered by God in accord with his wish and not answered with a view to his salvation? If I give the example of some person or other, perhaps you will say to me, "You call that man evil, but he was righteous; if he weren't righteous, his prayer wouldn't have been heard by God." I shall propose a

9. "Sacrament" here seems to be understood as "mystery."

person of whose evil and wickedness no one has any doubt. The devil himself asked for Job, and he received.[10] Wasn't it here as well that you heard regarding the devil that *he who commits sin is from the devil* (3:8), not because he created him but because he imitates him?[11] Wasn't it said of him, *He did not stand in the truth* (Jn 8:44)? Isn't he that ancient serpent who, by way of the woman, gave the first man something poisonous to take?[12] Isn't it he also who provided a woman for that very same Job, by whom he wouldn't be consoled but tempted?[13] The devil himself asked that the holy man be tempted, and he received. The Apostle asked that the goad of the flesh be removed from him, and he didn't receive. But the Apostle's prayer was answered in a better way than the devil's, for the Apostle was answered with a view to his salvation, even if not in accord with his wish, while the devil was answered in accord with his wish but with a view to his condemnation. For he who had to be tempted was yielded up, so that in the process of being proven he would be tormented. But this is something, brothers, that we find not only in the old books[14] but also in the gospel. Demons asked the Lord, when he was going to cast them out of a man, to allow them to go into swine.[15] Wouldn't the Lord have been able to tell them not to go there? For, if he were unwilling, they wouldn't have rebelled against the king of heaven and earth. Yet he sent the demons into the swine for the sake of a certain mystery and following a certain plan, so as to demonstrate that the devil lords it over those who lead the life of swine. Was the prayer of the demons answered, then, and did that of the Apostle go unanswered? Or should we instead say with greater truth that the Apostle's prayer was indeed answered while that of the demons was unanswered? The wish of the ones was accomplished, while the other's wellbeing[16] was perfected.

---

10. See Jb 1:11-12.
11. See V,2.
12. See Gn 3:1-6.
13. See Jb 2:9.
14. "Old books": *veteribus libris*. Augustine often refers to the Old Testament in this way in his writings.
15. See Lk 8:32.
16. "Wellbeing": *sanitas*. This can also mean "health" and even "salvation." Augustine probably intends the ambiguity. See also 8 below, where physical health is clearly intended.

8. In accordance with this we must understand that God provides for our salvation even if he doesn't comply with our wish. For what if you ask for what is hurtful to you, and the physician knows that it is hurtful to you? For it isn't a matter of the physician's not answering your request when, perhaps, you ask for cold water and, if it is beneficial, he gives it at once, and, if it isn't beneficial, he doesn't give it. Has he answered your request, or has he instead, by contravening your wish, been responsible for your wellbeing?

Let charity be in you, therefore, brothers; let it be in you, and be secure. And when what you ask for isn't given you, your prayer is being heard, but you are unaware of it. There are many who have been given over to their own hands by reason of their wickedness. The Apostle says of them, *God handed them over to the desires of their heart* (Rom 1:24). Someone has asked for a large sum of money; by reason of his wickedness he has received it. When he didn't have it, he wasn't particularly anxious; he began to have it and became the prey of someone more powerful. He who was under nobody's surveillance when he was poor, who wanted to have the resources to be under a thief's surveillance —hasn't his prayer been answered by reason of his wickedness? Learn to approach God in such a way that you entrust to your physician what he himself knows that he should do. You confess your illness and let him apply his medicine. You simply maintain charity. For he wants to cut, he wants to burn. If you cry out, and your prayer isn't heard during the cutting, during the burning and the pain, he knows how far the putrescence has gone. You want him to withdraw his hand now, and he is attending to your wound at its deepest part; he knows how far he must go. He isn't answering your prayer in accord with your wish, but he is answering it with a view to your wellbeing.

Be assured, then, my brothers, that what the Apostle says is true: *For what we should pray for, as it behooves, we do not know, but the Spirit himself asks with unutterable groans, because he himself asks on behalf of the saints* (Rom 8:26-27). What does *the Spirit himself asks on behalf of the saints* refer to if not to that very charity which was brought about in you through the Spirit? For that is why the same Apostle says, *The charity of God has been poured out in our hearts through the Holy Spirit, who has been given to us* (Rom 5:5). Charity itself groans, charity itself prays. Against it the one who gave it cannot stop his ears. Be secure; let charity ask, and there are God's ears. He doesn't do what you want, but he does what is necessary. Hence, *whatever we ask for*, it says, *we shall receive from him*. I have already said that, if you understand this with a view to salvation, it raises no question. If it isn't with a view to salvation, it raises a question, and a great one, which makes you a calumniator of the apostle Paul. *Whatever we ask for we shall receive from him, because we are keeping his commandments, and we are doing what is pleasing to him in his sight. In his sight*—within, where he sees.

9. And what are his commandments? *This is his commandment*, he says, *that we believe in the name of his Son Jesus Christ and love one another* (3:23). You see that this is his commandment. You see that he who acts against this commandment commits sin, which no one has who is born from God. *Just as he gave us his commandment* (3:23)—that we love one another. *And he who keeps his commandment* (3:24): you see that nothing else is imposed upon us except to love one another. *And he who keeps his commandment abides in him and he in him. And this is how we know that he is abiding in us—from the Spirit that he gave us*. (3:24) Isn't it clear that the Holy Spirit produces this in a person—that love and charity should be in him? Is what the apostle Paul says not clear—*The charity of God has been poured out in our hearts through the Holy Spirit, who has been given to us*? For he was speaking of charity, and he said that we must question our heart in God's presence. *If our heart does not think badly*—that is, if it confesses that whatever happens in a good work happens from love of one's brother. When he was speaking of the commandment he also added this and said, *This is his commandment, that we believe in the name of his Son Jesus Christ and love one another. And he who carries out his commandment abides in him and he in him. This is how we know that he is abiding in us—from the Spirit that he gave us*. If you have found that you have charity, you have the Spirit of God in order to understand, for this is something that is absolutely necessary.

10. In the first days the Holy Spirit fell upon the believers, and they spoke in tongues that they hadn't learned, as the Spirit gave them to speak.[17] These signs were appropriate for the time. For it was necessary that the Holy Spirit be signified thus in all tongues, because the gospel of God was going to traverse all tongues throughout the earth.[18] That was the sign that was given, and it passed. Is it expected now of those upon whom a hand is imposed, so that they may receive the Holy Spirit, that they speak in tongues?[19] Or, when we imposed our hand upon those infants,[20] was any one of you paying attention to see if they would speak in tongues? And, when he saw them not speaking in tongues, was there any one of you with a heart so perverse as to say, "They didn't receive the Holy Spirit, for, if they had received him, they would be speaking in tongues in the same way as happened then"? If, therefore, there is no testimony now by way of these miracles to the presence of the Holy Spirit, how does anyone know that he has received the Holy Spirit?

Let one question one's heart. If a person loves his brother, the Spirit of God is abiding in him. Let him look, let him probe himself before God's eyes. Let him see if there is in him a love of peace and unity, a love of the Church spread throughout the earth. Let him be attentive not only to loving the brother who is before him and upon whom he is intent, for there are many brothers of ours whom we do not see, and we are joined to them in the unity of the Spirit. Why should it surprise us that they aren't with us? We are in one body; we have one head in heaven.

Brothers, our eyes don't see each other as though they don't know each other. Don't they know each other in the charity of the body's structure? So that you may know that they know each other in the conjunction of charity, when both are open, it isn't permitted for the left one not to look at what the

---

17. See Acts 2:1-11.
18. The same thought appears in Sermons 267,3; 269,1; 270,6; 271. A contrast with the Donatists, who speak only Latin and Punic (see II,3), is implicit in the notion that the Catholic Church speaks all tongues.
19. Here Augustine chooses to link the baptismal imposition of the hand (note the singular) with the gift of the Spirit, whereas in III,5.12 he connects that gift with the baptismal anointing. Neither one need exclude the other.
20. As in I,5, the "infants" (*infantibus*) are such in terms of the faith. Speaking in tongues would have been an improbable effect of baptism.

right one is looking at. Direct the right one's ray[21] apart from the other, if you can. They go together; they are focused together. The gaze[22] is one; the positions are diverse. If, then, all those who love God with you share your one gaze, do not give thought to the fact that you are separated corporeally and spatially: together you have fixed the pupil of your heart's eye on the light of truth.

Therefore, if you want to know that you have received the Spirit, question your heart, lest perhaps you have the sacrament and don't have the sacrament's power.[23] Question your heart: if the love of your brother is there, be secure. There can be no love without the Spirit of God, because Paul cries out, *The charity of God has been poured out in our hearts through the Holy Spirit, who has been given to us.*

11. *Beloved, do not believe every spirit* (4:1). That is why he said, *This is how we know that he is abiding in us—from the Spirit that he gave us.* Pay heed to how the Spirit himself is known: *Beloved, do not believe every spirit, but test the spirits if they are from God* (4:1). And who is it that tests spirits? My brothers, he has proposed something difficult; it is good for us that he himself says how to make the distinction. He is going to say, "Don't fear." But first look, pay heed. See here expressed how the vain heretics calumniate us. Pay heed; see what he says: *Beloved, do not believe every spirit, but test the spirits if they are from God.*

The Holy Spirit is referred to as water in the gospel, when the Lord cries out and says, *If anyone thirsts, let him come to me and drink; he who believes in me, streams of living water shall flow from his belly* (Jn 7:37-38). The evangelist, however, made clear of whom he was speaking, for he continued and said, *But he said this of the Spirit, whom they were going to receive who were going to believe in him* (Jn 7:39). Why

---

21. "Direct the right one's ray": *dirige radium dextrum*. In Stoic theory the eyes direct rays toward the object that they are viewing. Augustine explains the theory in *The Literal Meaning of Genesis* VII,13,20-14,20. See also Rettig's note.

22. "Gaze": *intentio*, as in the following sentence.

23. The distinction between the sacrament and its power (*virtus*) would be elaborated in Scholastic theology, and in Scholastic terms the distinction would be between the *sacramentum tantum* and the *res tantum*. The present passage is a *locus classicus*. The distinction between water and the Spirit that is made in 11 below ("The water of the sacrament is one thing, therefore, and the water that signifies the Spirit of God is something else ... ") elaborates on what Augustine says here. For a brief but dense discussion of Augustine's theology in this regard see *Dictionnaire de Théologie Catholique* XIV/1.521-522.

didn't the Lord baptize many? But what did he say? *But the Spirit had not yet been given, because Jesus had not yet been glorified* (Jn 7:39). Because, then, they had baptism and hadn't yet received the Holy Spirit, whom the Lord sent from heaven on the day of Pentecost, the glorification of the Lord was awaited so that the Spirit might be given. And before he was glorified, and before he sent him, he nonetheless invited people to prepare themselves to receive the water of which he said, *If anyone thirsts, let him come to me and drink,* and, *He who believes in me, streams of living water shall flow from his belly.* What does *streams of living water* mean? What is that water? No one should question me; question the gospel. *But he said this*, he said, *of the Spirit, whom they were going to receive who were going to believe in him.*

The water of the sacrament is one thing, therefore, and the water that signifies the Spirit of God is something else. The water of the sacrament is visible; the water of the Spirit is invisible. The former washes the body and signifies what takes place in the soul; by the latter, the Spirit, the soul itself is cleansed and nourished. This is the very Spirit of God, whom heretics and whoever cut themselves off from the Church cannot have. And whoever don't openly cut themselves off but are cut off by wickedness, and are whirled about within like chaff and are not grain, don't have this Spirit. This Spirit is signified by the Lord by the word *water.* And we heard from this epistle: *Do not believe every spirit*; and the words of Solomon bear testimony: *Abstain from alien water* (Prv 9:18 LXX). What does *water* mean? A spirit. Does water always signify a spirit? Not always, but in certain passages it signifies a spirit,[24] in certain passages it signifies baptism, in certain passages it signifies peoples, in certain passages it signifies counsel.[25] In a certain passage you have it said, *Counsel is a font of life for those who possess it* (Prv 16:22). Hence, in different passages of the scriptures the term *water* signifies different things. Yet you have heard now that the Holy Spirit is referred to as water not by our interpretation but by gospel testimony, where it is said, *But he said this of the Spirit, whom they*

---

24. As becomes apparent in this passage, water can symbolize either the Holy Spirit or another spirit, either good or bad.

25. We have an indication here of the great flexibility that could be found in the allegorical method of interpreting scripture. In illustrating the different meanings of water in the following lines, however, Augustine doesn't show how it symbolizes peoples (*populos*).

were going to receive who were going to believe in him. If, then, the Holy Spirit is signified by the term *water*, and this epistle tells us, *Do not believe every spirit, but test the spirits if they are from God*, we should understand from there what was said: *Abstain from foreign water, and do not drink from an alien font* (Prv 9:18 LXX). What does *Do not drink from an alien font* mean? You should not believe in an alien spirit.

12. What remains, then, is a way of testing whether a spirit is of God. [John] did indeed provide a sign, and it is perhaps difficult. Let us see it nonetheless. We are going to return to charity. It is that which teaches us, because it is the anointing. Yet what does he say here? *Test the spirits if they are from God, because many false prophets have gone out into the world* (4:1). All the heretics and all the schismatics are already there. How, then, do I test a spirit? Here is what follows: *This is how the Spirit of God is known* (4:2). Perk up the ears of your heart. We were making an effort and saying, "Who knows? Who can distinguish?" Well, he is about to tell of the sign. *This is how the Spirit of God is known: every spirit that confesses that Jesus Christ has come in the flesh is from God. And every spirit that does not confess that Jesus Christ has come in the flesh is not from God. And he is the antichrist, of whom you heard that he was going to come, and he is now in this world.* (4:2-3) It is as though our ears are perked up to distinguish the spirits, and we have heard of such a thing from which we may distinguish nothing less. For what does he say? *Every spirit that confesses that Jesus Christ has come in the flesh is from God.* Is the spirit that is with the heretics from God, then, inasmuch as they confess that Jesus Christ has come in the flesh? At this point perhaps they rise up against us and say, "You don't have a spirit from God, but we confess that Jesus Christ has come in the flesh. But he denies that those who don't confess that Jesus Christ has come in the flesh have the Spirit of God." Ask the Arians: they confess that Jesus Christ has come in the flesh.[26] Ask the Eunomians: they confess that Jesus Christ has come in the flesh.[27] Ask the Macedonians:

---

26. The Arians, who took their name from Arius (d. c. 336), a priest of Alexandria, denied that the Son was equal to the Father. Augustine seems to have them in mind in II,5.

27. The Eunomians, who took their name from Eunomius (d. c. 395), bishop of Cyzicus, were one of the many variants of Arianism. In addition to holding the inferiority of the Son to the Father, they also insisted that the Father was completely intelligible to human beings.

they confess that Jesus Christ has come in the flesh.[28] Question the Cataphrygians: they confess that Jesus Christ has come in the flesh.[29] Question the Novatians: they confess that Jesus Christ has come in the flesh.[30] Do all these heresies, then, have the Spirit of God? Aren't they false prophets, then? Is there no falsehood there, then? Is there no deception? They are indeed antichrists who went out from us but weren't from us.

13. What, then, do we do? How do we distinguish? Be attentive. Let us go together in heart, and let us knock.[31] Charity herself is keeping watch, because it is she who is going to knock and she who is going to open. Now you will understand in the name of our Lord Jesus Christ. You have already heard previously that it was said, *He who denies that Jesus Christ has come in the flesh, he is the antichrist.*[32] And we asked there who would deny, because neither do we deny nor do they deny.[33] And we found that there are certain ones who deny by their deeds, and we used the testimony of the Apostle, who says, *For they confess that they know God, but by their deeds they deny him* (Ti 1:16).[34] And so we too now look at deeds, not at speech.

Which is the spirit that isn't from God? *The one that denies that Jesus Christ has come in the flesh.* And which is the spirit that is from God? *The one that confesses that Jesus Christ has come in the flesh.* Who is it that confesses that Jesus Christ has come in the flesh? Ah, brothers, let us pay attention to actions, not to the sound of the tongue. Let us ask why Christ has come in the flesh, and we find who denies that he has come in the flesh. For, if you pay attention to tongues, you are going to hear many heresies confessing that Christ has come in the flesh, but the truth convicts them. Why did Christ come in the flesh? Wasn't he God? Wasn't it written of him, *In the beginning was the Word, and the Word was with God, and the*

---

28. The Macedonians were so called after Macedonius, a bishop of Constantinople (d. c. 362). Whether correctly or not, his name was attached to the heresy that denied the divinity of the Holy Spirit. Its adherents were otherwise known as Pneumatomachians, or Spirit-fighters.
29. The Cataphrygians were another name for the Montanists, who originated in Phrygia in the second century. The Cataphrygians believed that in some sense the Son had been superseded by the Holy Spirit.
30. The Novatians took their name from the Roman priest Novatian (d. c. 258); they were a schismatic movement rather than a heresy and were notable for their moral rigor.
31. See Mt 7:7.
32. This seems to be a conflation of 2:22 and 4:3.
33. See above 12.
34. See III,8.

Word was God (Jn 1:1)? Hasn't he provided food for his angels, and doesn't he provide food for his angels? Didn't he come here in such a way as not to leave there? Didn't he go up in such a way as not to abandon us? Why, then, did he come in the flesh? Because we had to be shown the hope of resurrection. He was God, and he came in the flesh, for God couldn't die, but flesh could die. He came in the flesh, therefore, in order to die for us. But how did he die for us? *Greater charity than this no one has, than to lay down his life for his friends* (Jn 15:13). It was charity, then, that led him to the flesh. Whoever doesn't have charity, therefore, denies that Christ has come in the flesh. At this point now, ask all heretics: "Did Christ come in the flesh?" "He came; I believe it, I confess it." "In fact you are denying it." "How am I denying it? You hear that this is what I am saying." "In fact I convict you of denying it. You are saying it with your voice, you are denying it in your heart. You are saying it in words, you are denying it in deeds." "How," you say, "am I denying it in deeds?" "Because Christ came in the flesh in order to die for us. He died for us because he taught much charity. *Greater charity than this no one has, than to lay down his life for his friends.* You don't have charity because, for the sake of your honor, you cause divisions in unity. Understand from this, then, that the spirit is from God. Strike at and feel the earthen vessels[35] to see if perhaps they are broken and give back a bad sound. See if they sound whole; see if charity is there. You are removing yourself from the world's unity, you are dividing the Church with schisms, you are tearing to pieces the body of Christ. He came in the flesh so as to bring it together; you are crying out so as to scatter it." The spirit of God, then, is he who says that Jesus has come in the flesh, who says it not with his tongue but by his deeds, who says it not with words but by loving.[36] But he isn't the spirit of God who denies that Christ has come in the flesh: and he denies it not with his tongue but by his life, not with words but by deeds. It is clear, then, how we may know, brothers. There are many who are within who are partly within; no one is without unless he is truly without.

14. Indeed, so that you may know that he has referred to deeds, [John] says, *And every spirit that dissolves the fact that Christ has come in the*

---

35. See 2 Cor 4:7.
36. "Not with words but by loving": *non sonando sed amando.*

flesh is not from God (4:2-3).[37] It is understood that he dissolves by his deeds. What is he showing you? The one who denies, because he said *dissolves*. He came to gather, you came to dissolve. You want to sunder the members of Christ. How do you not deny that Christ has come in the flesh, you who break up the Church of God that he gathered together? You have come against Christ, therefore; you are an antichrist. You may be within, you may be without; you are an antichrist. But when you are within, you are hidden; when you are without, you are manifested. You dissolve Jesus, and you deny that he has come in the flesh. You aren't from God. That is why it says in the gospel, *He who dissolves one of these least commandments and teaches thus shall be called least in the kingdom of heaven* (Mt 5:19). What does it mean to be dissolved? What does it mean to be taught? Dissolving pertains to deeds, and teaching pertains more or less to words. *You steal, you who preach that no one should steal* (Rom 2:21). He who steals, then, dissolves by a deed, and he more or less teaches thus. *He shall be called least in the kingdom of heaven*—that is, in the Church of this time. Of him it is written: *Do what they say, but do not do what they do* (Mt 23:3). *But he who does and teaches thus shall be called great in the kingdom of heaven* (Mt 5:19). And, by saying what he said here, *does*, he spoke against what was in the other passage, *dissolves*—that is, doesn't do and teaches thus. He who doesn't do, then, dissolves. What does he teach us except that we should question deeds, not believe words?

The obscurity of these matters obliges us to say many things, especially so that what the Lord deigns to reveal may reach the slower brothers as well, because all have been purchased with Christ's blood. And I fear that this epistle may not be finished during these days, as I had promised. But (and this is pleasing to the Lord) it is better to save what remains than to burden hearts with too much food.

---

37. This rendering of the passage is almost entirely different from previous renderings because of the use of the verb *solvere* ("dissolve") instead of *negare* ("deny"), which translates a variant in the original Greek text. See the note in Browne. Still another version, using both *solvere* and *negare* and omitting "spirit," occurs in VII,2. Perhaps an equally good translation would be "do away with."

Seventh Homily

1. This world is to all the faithful who are seeking their homeland what the desert was to the people of Israel. They were indeed wandering the whole time and in search of their homeland, but, since God was leading them, they couldn't go astray.[1] God's command was their way. For when they went around for forty years, the journey itself is made up of very few stages,[2] and this is known to all. They experienced delays because they were being exercised, not because they were being forsaken. What God promises us, then, is an ineffable sweetness and a good, as scripture says, and you have often heard us referring to *what the eye has not seen nor the ear heard, nor has it entered into the heart of man* (1 Cor 2:9). We are being exercised by temporal labors, however, and we are being educated by the trials of the present life. But, if you don't want to die of thirst in this desert, drink charity. This is the fountain that the Lord wanted to set there, lest we grow weary on the way, and we shall drink of it more abundantly when we come to our homeland.

A little while ago the gospel was read. What else should I say of the words with which the reading concluded except that you heard about charity? For we have established a contract with our God in the Prayer that, if we want him to forgive our sins, we should also forgive the sins that have been committed against us.[3] But there is no forgiveness apart from charity. Remove charity from the heart and it holds onto hatred and cannot forgive. Let charity be there and it forgives with a sense of security and is not made narrow. See if this entire epistle, which we have undertaken to preach on, commends anything else than this one charity itself. Nor is there reason to fear that, by mentioning it often, it may become distasteful. For what is loved if charity becomes distasteful?

---

1. "Wandering ... go astray": *errabant ... errare*. While Augustine uses the same verb, it is clear that he means it in two different senses.
2. Somewhat strangely, the perfect "went around" (*circumierunt*) is followed by the present "is made up" (*conficitur*).
3. See Mt 6:12. I have translated *in oratione* as "in the Prayer" rather than simply as "in prayer" in order to specify the Lord's Prayer—which is being alluded to here—and to emphasize the singular place that it occupied in the early Christian mentality.

Since[4] it is by charity that other things are loved well, how ought it to be loved itself? It is something, then, which must never forsake our heart, nor should it forsake our mouth.

2. *Little children*, he says, *you are already from God, and you have conquered him* (4:4). Whom but the Antichrist? For he had said previously, *Everyone who dissolves Jesus Christ and denies that he has come in the flesh is not from God* (4:3).[5] If you recall, we have explained that all those who violate charity deny that Jesus Christ has come in the flesh.[6] For, apart from charity, it wasn't necessary for Jesus to come. For it is that charity which is commended to us which he himself also commends in the gospel: *Greater love than this no one can have than to lay down his life for his friends* (Jn 15:13). How could the Son of God lay down his life for us if he weren't clothed in the flesh in which he could die? Whoever violates charity, then, let the tongue say what it will, denies by his life that Christ has come in the flesh, and he is an antichrist, wherever he may be, wherever he may enter.[7] But what does he say to those who are citizens of that homeland for which we yearn? *You have conquered him.* And how have they conquered? *Because he who is in you is greater than him who is in this world* (4:4). Lest they attribute their victory to their own strength and be conquered by the arrogance of pride (for the devil conquers whomever he has made proud), what does he say who wants them to maintain their humility? *You have conquered him.* Every person who hears *You have conquered* lifts up his head, stiffens his neck and wants to be praised. Don't extol yourself. See who has conquered in you. Why have you conquered? *Because he who is in you is greater than him who is in this world.* Be humble; carry your Lord; be the beast of burden of him who sits upon you.[8] It is good for you that he guides and that he leads. For, if you wouldn't have him sit upon you, you can stiffen your neck, you can

---

4. Reading *quia* instead of *qua*.
5. See VI,14 and note 37.
6. See VI,12-14, esp. 13.
7. "Wherever he may enter": *quocumque intraverit*—i.e. even if he enters a church, *pace* Rettig ("wherever he comes"). See 6 below: "Although they may enter the basilicas ... " (*quamvis intrent basilicas*).
8. See Mt 21:5-7 par. The image is a beautiful and unusual one.

strike with your feet. Woe to you if you are without a guide, because that freedom sends you to the beasts to be devoured.[9]

3. *They are of the world* (4:5). Who? Antichrists. You have already heard who they are. And, if you aren't one, you know them. But whoever is one doesn't know it. *They are of the world; hence, they speak of the world, and the world listens to them* (4:5). Who are they who speak of the world? Notice who are against charity. See, you have heard the Lord saying, *If you forgive people their sins, your heavenly Father will forgive you your sins. But, if you do not forgive them, neither will your Father forgive you your sins.* (Mt 6:14-15) This is a word of truth. Or, if it isn't the truth that is speaking, contradict it. If you are a Christian and believe Christ, he himself said, *I am the truth* (Jn 14:6). This is a true word; it is solid. Now listen to the persons who speak of the world: "And aren't you going to vindicate yourself, and is he going to say that he did this to you? Indeed, you should make it clear that he is dealing with a man." These things are said every day. Those who say these things are speaking of the world, and the world listens to them. Nor does anyone say these things apart from those who love the world, neither are these things listened to except by those who love the world. And you have heard that he who loves the world and neglects charity denies that Jesus has come in the flesh. Did the Lord himself do that in the flesh? When he was being beaten, did he want to be vindicated? When he was hanging on the cross, didn't he say, *Father, forgive them, because they do not know what they are doing* (Lk 23:34)? But, if he who had power didn't threaten, why do you threaten? Why do you rage, who are subject to another power? He died because he wanted to, and he didn't threaten. You don't know when you will die, and you threaten!

4. *We are from God* (4:6). Let us see why. See if there is any reason apart from charity. *We are from God. He who knows God listens to us. He who is not from God does not listen to us. This is how we know the spirit of truth and of error* (4:6), because he who listens to us has the spirit of

---

9. This violent image of hungry beasts (*bestias*) that are ready to devour the Christian who abuses his freedom stands in contrast to the preceding pacific image of the beast of burden (*iumentum*) that symbolizes the Christian who has submitted his freedom to Christ.

truth; he who doesn't listen to us has the spirit of error. Let us see what he advises, and let us listen to him as he advises in the spirit of truth—not to the antichrists, not to the lovers of the world, not to the world—if we have been born from God. *Beloved* follows what came before. See what that was: *We are from God. He who knows God listens to us. He who is not from God does not listen to us. This is how we know the spirit of truth and of error.* Now that has made us attentive, because he who knows God is the very one who is listening, whereas he who doesn't know him isn't listening, and this is the distinction between the spirits of truth and of error. Let us see what advice he is going to give, about which we ought to listen to him. *Beloved, let us love one another* (4:7). Why? Because a human being is giving the advice? *Because love is from God* (4:7). He has commended love highly, because he said that it is from God. He is going to say more; let us listen intently. Now he has said, *Love is from God, and everyone who loves has been born from God and knows God. He who does not love does not know God.* (4:7-8) Why? *Because God is love* (4:8). What more could be said, brothers? If nothing were said in praise of love in all the pages of this epistle, if nothing at all were said in the other pages of the scriptures, and this were the one and only thing that we heard from the voice of the Spirit of God, that *God is love*, we wouldn't have to look for anything else.

5. See now that to act against love is to act against God. Let no one say, "I'm sinning against a human being when I don't love my brother." Listen to this! "And a sin against a human being is easy. Against God alone I wouldn't sin." How don't you sin against God when you sin against love? *God is love.* Are we saying this? If we were the ones who said, *God is love*, perhaps one of you would be scandalized and would say, "What did he say? What did he want to say, that *God is love*? God gave love. God bestowed love." *Love is from God. God is love.* There, brothers, you have the scriptures of God. This epistle is canonical; it is read among all the nations; it is preserved by the authority of the whole world; it has built up the whole world. Here you are listening to the Spirit of God: *God is love.* Now, if you dare, act against God, and don't love your brother.

6. How, then, could it be a short while ago, *Love is from God*, and now, *Love is God*?[10] For God is Father and Son and Holy Spirit. The Son is God from God, the Holy Spirit is God from God, and these three are one God, not three gods. If the Son is God and the Holy Spirit is God, and he loves him in whom the Holy Spirit dwells, then love is God, but it is God because it is from God. For you have each one in the epistle—both *Love is from God* and *Love is God*. Of the Father alone scripture cannot say that he is from God. But when you hear *from God*, either the Son or the Holy Spirit is understood. But, because the Apostle says, *The charity of God has been poured out in our hearts through the Holy Spirit, who has been given to us* (Rom 5:5), we should understand that in love there is the Holy Spirit. For the Holy Spirit is he whom the wicked cannot receive. He is that font of which scripture says, *Let the font of your water be your own, and let no stranger have a part in you* (Prv 5:16-17). For all those who don't love God are strangers; they are antichrists. And, although they may enter the basilicas, they cannot be numbered among the children of God; that font of life isn't theirs. A wicked person can also have baptism. A wicked person can also have prophecy. We have found that King Saul had prophecy: he was pursuing the holy David, and he was filled with the spirit of prophecy and began to prophesy.[11] A wicked person can also receive the sacrament of the body and blood of the Lord, for of such persons it is said, *He who eats and drinks unworthily eats and drinks judgment to himself* (1 Cor 11:29). A wicked person can also have Christ's name—that is, a wicked person can also be called a Christian. Of them it is said, *They have polluted the name of their God* (Ez 36:20). A wicked person, therefore, can also have all these sacraments, but a person cannot be wicked and also have charity. This, then, is a particular gift; it is the unique font. The Spirit of God exhorts you to drink from it; the Spirit of God exhorts you to drink from himself.

10. Whereas previously the order of the words had been *Deus dilectio est* ("God is love"), here and in what immediately follows it is *dilectio Deus est* ("love is God").
   On what follows see *The Trinity* II,1,2 (the Father alone is not from God); V,8,9 (there are not three gods but one God).
11. See 1 S 19. How Saul, who persecuted David, could have had a prophetic spirit was clearly a matter of some confusion in the ancient Church, and Augustine addresses the problem in *Miscellany of Questions in Response to Simplician* II,1.

7. *This is how the love of God has been manifested in us* (4:9). See, we have an exhortation to love God. Would we be able to love him if he didn't love us first? If we were sluggish in loving, let us not be sluggish in returning love. He loved us first; that isn't how we love. He loved us when we were wicked, but he did away with our wickedness; he loved us when we were wicked, but he didn't gather us together for the sake of wickedness. He loved us when we were sick, but he visited us in order to heal us. *God is love*, therefore. *This is how the love of God has been manifested in us, that he sent his only-begotten Son into this world, so that we might live through him* (4:9). As the Lord himself said, *Greater love no one can have than to lay down his life for his friends*, and the love of Christ is proved in us because he died for us. How is the love of the Father[12] proved in us? Because he sent his only Son to die for us. And so the apostle Paul says, *How did he, who did not spare his own Son but handed him over for all of us, not also give us all things with him?* (Rom 8:32) See, the Father handed over Christ and Judas handed him over. Does the deed not somehow seem the same? Judas is a betrayer.[13] Is the Father a betrayer then, too? "By no means," you say. I don't say this, but the Apostle says it: *Who did not spare his own Son but handed him over for all of us*. The Father handed him over, and he himself handed himself over. The same Apostle says, *Who loved me and handed himself over for me* (Gal 2:20). If the Father handed over the Son, and the Son handed over himself, what did Judas do? A handing-over[14] was carried out by the Father, a handing-over was carried out by the Son, a handing-over was carried out by Judas: one thing was carried out. But what is the thing that distinguishes among the Father handing over his Son, the Son handing over himself, and the disciple Judas handing over his master? That the Father and the Son did this in charity, but that Judas did it in betrayal. You see that it isn't what a person does that must be taken into consideration but with what mind and will he does it. We find God the

---

12. *Dilectio patri* ("love to the Father"), which the Latin text has, must be a mistake; I have substituted *patris* ("of the Father").
13. "Betrayer": *traditor*; "hand over": *tradere*.
14. "Handing-over": *traditio*.

Father in the same act in which we find Judas; we bless the Father and detest Judas. Why do we bless the Father and detest Judas? We bless charity and detest wickedness. For how much was offered to the human race by Christ, who was handed over? Did Judas think of this, so that he would hand him over? God thought of our salvation, whereby we were redeemed, and Judas thought of the price for which he sold the Lord. The Son himself thought of the price that he paid for us, and Judas thought of the price that he received for his sale. A different intention, therefore, created different acts. Although there is one thing, if we survey it from the perspective of different intentions, we find that one is to be loved and the other is to be condemned, one is to be glorified and the other is to be detested. So much is charity worth! See that it alone distinguishes; see that people's deeds alone distinguish.

8. We have said this with respect to similar deeds. With respect to different deeds, we find [one] person made fierce by charity and [another person] made flattering by wickedness. A father beats a boy and a slave dealer flatters him. If you set forth the two things, blows and flattery, who would not choose the flattery and avoid the blows? If you pay heed to the persons, it is charity that beats and wickedness that flatters. See what we are commending, because people's deeds are indistinguishable apart from the root of charity. For there are many things which can come about that have a good appearance and don't proceed from the root of charity. After all, thorns also have flowers. There are some, however, that seem harsh and that seem rough, but they contribute to discipline under the guidance of charity. Once for all, then, a brief precept is given to you: Love, and do what you want.[15] If you are silent, be silent with love; if you cry out, cry out with love; if you chastise, chastise with love; if you spare, spare with love. The root of love must be within; nothing but good can come forth from this root.

---

15. "Love, and do what you want": *dilige, et quod vis fac*. This is certainly one of Augustine's most famous and oft-abused lines, but its true meaning is utterly clear in the context. From the phrase immediately preceding it ("Once for all … "), one has the impression that Augustine himself was aware that his formulation had a disconcerting tone.

9. *Love consists in this. This is how the love of God has been manifested in us, that God sent his only-begotten Son into this world, so that we might live through him. Love consists in this, not that we have loved, but that he has loved us.* (4:9-10) We did not love him first, for it was so that we might love him that he loved us. *And he sent his Son as the atoner for our sins* (4:10). "Atoner" means "sacrificer."[16] He sacrificed for our sins. Where did he find the offering? Where did he find the pure victim that he wanted to offer? He found no other one: he offered himself.[17] *Beloved, if God has so loved us, we must also love one another* (4:11). *Peter*, he said, *do you love me?* And he said, *I love you. Feed my sheep.* (Jn 21:15-17)

10. *No one has ever seen God* (4:12). He is an invisible reality; he must be sought not with the eye but with the heart. But just as, if we wanted to see the sun, we would cleanse the eye of our body, whereby light can be seen, we should cleanse the eye whereby God can be seen if we want to see God. Where is that eye? Listen to the gospel: *Blessed are the clean of heart, for they shall see God* (Mt 5:8). But let no one imagine God for himself in keeping with the concupiscence of his eyes. For he makes a huge shape for himself; or he stretches out some immeasurable vastness through space, as though spreading across open places—as much as he can—the light that he sees with these eyes; or he makes for himself some old man of, as it were, venerable aspect.[18] Do not think of these. This is what you should think of if you want to see God: *God is love.* What sort of countenance does love have? What sort of shape does it have? What sort of height does it have? What sort of feet does it have? What sort of hands does it have? No one can say. Yet it has feet, for they lead to the Church.[19] It has hands, for they stretch out to the poor person. It has eyes, for that is how he who is in need is understood: *Blessed*, it says, *is he who under-*

---

16. ' "Atoner" means "sacrificer" ': *litatorem, sacrificatorem. Litator* seems to be quite a rare word.

17. "Offering ... victim ... to offer ... offered": *hostiam ... victimam ... offerre ... obtulit.*

18. Augustine himself had once conceived of God in just such physical and anthropomorphic ways, as he acknowledges in *Confessions* V,10,20; VII,1,1-2.

19. The question is whether Augustine means a church building or the universal Church or both. Given his strong awareness that there are many whose feet have brought them to the building but who have no real engagement, he would seem to be speaking primarily of the universal Church without excluding a given church building. For a rather poignant description of those who filled (or failed to fill) the church at Hippo, and their various degrees of commitment, see Van der Meer 169-177.

stands concerning the needy and the poor (Ps 41:1). It has ears, of which the Lord says, *He who has ears to hear, let him hear* (Lk 8:8). These aren't distinct members occupying space, but he who has charity sees everything all at once with his understanding. Dwell there, and you shall be indwelled. Abide there, and you shall be abided in.

For, my brothers, who loves what he doesn't see? But why, when charity is praised, are you excited and applaud and praise?[20] What have I shown you? Have I produced some colorful things? Have I brought out gold and silver? Have I dug up gems from treasure chests? What have I set before your eyes that is like that? Has my countenance changed as I speak? I am wearing flesh. I have the same aspect that I had when I came in; you have the same aspect that you had when you came in. Charity is being praised, and you shout. You see nothing, to be sure. But it should please you to observe it in your heart just as it pleases you when you praise it. Pay attention to what I am saying, brothers. I am exhorting you, as much as the Lord allows, with regard to a great treasure. If you were shown a small finely-wrought gilt vessel that had been carefully made, and it was alluring to your eyes and attractive to your heart, and the artificer's workmanship pleased you, along with the weight of the silver and the sheen of the metal, wouldn't one of you say, "O, if only I had that vessel"? And you would say it to no avail, for it wasn't within your means. Or, if someone wanted to have it, he would think about stealing it from someone else's house. Charity is being praised to you. If it is pleasing, have it, possess it. There is no need to steal it from anyone else. There is no need for you to think of buying it: it is free. Take it, embrace it: nothing is sweeter than it. If this is what it is like when it is being spoken of, what must it be like when it is had?

11. If any one of you wants to maintain charity, brothers, do not, above all, think of it as depressing and lackluster, as not even to be maintained with a certain mildness—certainly not mildness!—but with laxity and neglect. That isn't how it is maintained. You shouldn't think that you

---

20. Here and in what follows Augustine is commenting on his congregation's boisterous response to his previous words on charity. See also III,11.

love your slave when you don't beat him, or that you love your son when you don't discipline him, or that you love your neighbor when you don't correct him. That isn't charity but indifference. Charity should be afire to correct and improve. But if there is good behavior, it should delight; if there is bad, it should be improved, corrected. Don't love the error in a person but the person: God made the person; the person himself made the error. Love what God made; don't love what the person himself made. When you love the one, you take away the other; when you love the one, you improve the other. But even if you are occasionally harsh, let it be on account of the love that corrects.

This is why charity is shown by the dove that came upon the Lord.[21] That form of a dove, in which form the Holy Spirit came, whereby charity was poured out upon us: why was this? A dove has no bile,[22] yet it fights for its nest with beak and wings; it is harsh without bitterness. A father is also like that; when he punishes his child, he punishes him for the sake of discipline. As I said,[23] a seducer flatters with bitterness in order to sell, while a father chastises without bile in order to correct; be like that to everyone. See, brothers, a great warning, a great rule: whoever has or wants to have children, or if he has decided not to have children at all in a fleshly way but desires to have them spiritually: Who is it that doesn't correct his child? Who is it upon whom his father wouldn't impose discipline?[24] And yet he seems to be harsh. Love is harsh; charity is harsh. It is harsh in a kind of way without bile—like a dove, not like a crow.

Hence it comes to mind, my brothers, to tell you that those who violate charity have created a schism.[25] As they hate charity itself, they also hate the dove. But the dove convicts them: he comes from heaven, the heavens are opened, and he rests on the Lord's head. Why? So that he would hear: *He is the one who baptizes* (Jn 1:33). Retreat, plunderers! Retreat, usurpers of Christ's possession! You have dared to affix the Master's

---

21. See Mt 3:16.
22. Bile was one of the four humors that the ancients believed were responsible for one's disposition. Bile, or choler, was the source of anger.
23. In 8 above.
24. See Heb 12:7.
25. Augustine is referring to the Donatists in what remains of the homily.

titles [of ownership] to your own possessions, where you want to hold sway. He knows his own titles; he claims his possession for himself; he doesn't erase the titles but enters in and possesses. Thus, for the one who comes to the Catholic Church,[26] baptism isn't erased, lest the Ruler's title be erased. But what happens in the Catholic Church? The title is recognized; the Owner enters under his own titles, where the plunderer had entered under another's titles.[27]

---

26. "Catholic Church": *catholicam*. Augustine sometimes refers to the orthodox Church as the *catholica*, which means "universal" and which emphasizes the contrast with Donatist particularity. The term appears again in the following sentence.
27. Donatists rebaptized those who entered Donatism from Catholicism, because they considered Catholic baptism invalid. Catholics, however, did not rebaptize Donatists in the same circumstances, because they held that Donatists truly possessed sacramental baptism, albeit by usurpation.

Eighth Homily

1. Love is a sweet word but a sweeter deed. We can't always speak of it, for we have many things to do, and our different activities distract us, so that there is no opportunity for our tongue always to be speaking of love. But one can always keep what one cannot always speak about. For example, the Alleluia that we now sing: are we always doing this? Scarcely for the space of an hour—rather, only for a small part of it—are we singing Alleluia, and we turn to something else. But, as you already know, Alleluia means "praise God." He who praises God with his tongue cannot always do so. He who praises God with his behavior *can* always do so. The works of mercy, the warmth of charity, the holiness of devotion, the incorruption of chastity, the modesty of sobriety: these things must always be kept whether we are in public or at home or in the presence of others or in our room or speaking or being silent or doing something or doing nothing. These things must always be kept, because all these virtues which I have named are within. Who is sufficient to name them all? They are like the army of a general who occupies his seat within your mind. For, just as a general does through his army whatever pleases him, so the Lord Jesus Christ, when he begins to dwell in our inner man (that is, in our mind through faith[1]), uses these virtues as his ministers. And through these virtues, which cannot be seen by the eyes and are nonetheless praised when they are named (but they wouldn't be praised unless they were loved, nor would they be loved unless they were seen; and if indeed they wouldn't be loved unless they were seen, they are seen by another eye—that is, by the heart's inner gaze)—through these invisible virtues our members are moved visibly. The feet for walking: but where? Where a good will, which soldiers for a good general, moves them. The hands for working: but for what? For what charity, which has been inspired within by the Holy Spirit, commands. Our members, then, are seen when they are moved; he who commands within isn't seen. And

---

1. See Eph 3:17.

who would command within—almost only he knows who commands, and he to whom the command is given within.

2. You were listening a short while ago, when the gospel was being read—certainly if you had an ear not only of the body but also of the heart. What did it say? *Beware of practicing your righteousness in the presence of men, in order to be seen by them* (Mt 6:1). Does this mean that, whatever good we do, we should conceal it from the eyes of men and fear that it be seen? If you are afraid that people will see you, you will have no imitators; therefore you should be seen.[2] But that isn't why you should allow yourself to be seen. The goal of your joy mustn't be there, nor the end of your gladness, that you should think that you have acquired the whole fruit of your good work when you have been seen and praised. That is nothing. Disdain yourself when you are praised. Let him who works through you be praised in you. Don't accomplish whatever good you do for your own praise, then, but for the praise of him from whom you have the means to do good. From yourself you have the means to do bad, from God you have the means to do good. On the other hand, see how absurd wicked persons are. The good that they do they want to attribute to themselves; if what they do is bad, they want to blame God. Turn around this distorted and absurd anomaly, which in a certain way puts things upside down, putting down what is up and up what is down. Do you want to put God down and yourself up? You are casting yourself down and not raising yourself up, for he is always above. What then? Is the good yours and the bad God's? On the contrary, this is what you should say, if you want to speak more truly: The bad is mine and the good is his, and the good that I do is his good, for whatever bad I do is from me. This confession strengthens the heart and provides the foundation of love.

For, if we ought to conceal our good works lest they be seen by men, where are those words of the Lord in that sermon that he gave on the mount? When he said this,[3] this is what he said there shortly before: *Let your good works shine before men* (Mt 5:16). And he didn't stop there,

---

2. This sentence is an answer to the previous question, but it in turn receives a response in what follows.
3. I.e., what he said in Mt 6:1.

he didn't conclude there, but he added: *And let them glorify your Father, who is in heaven* (Mt 5:16).

And what did the Apostle say? *But I was unknown by sight to the churches of Judea that are in Christ, but they only heard that he who once persecuted us is now preaching the faith that he was once ravaging, and they glorified God in me* (Gal 1:22-24). See how he too, because he was known in that way, set his goal not at his own praise but at the praise of God. And, as far as pertains to him, the ravisher of the Church, the hostile persecutor, the wicked man—it is he himself who is confessing and not we who are reproaching him. Paul loves for his sins to be recounted by us, so that he who healed so grave a disease might be glorified. For the physician's hand cut and healed the great wound. The voice from heaven thrust down the persecutor and raised up a preacher; it killed Saul and brought Paul to life.[4] For Saul was the persecutor of a holy man.[5] It was from him that he had the name when he was persecuting Christians; afterwards, from Saul he became Paul.[6] What does Paul mean? "Little."[7] Therefore, when he was Saul he was proud, lofty; when he was Paul he was humble, little. That is why we say, "I'll see you a little later"—that is, after a little while.[8] Hear how little he became: *For I am the least of the apostles* (1 Cor 15:9); and in another place he says: *To me, the least of all the holy ones* (Eph 3:8). Thus among the apostles he was like the fringe of a garment, but the Church of the gentiles, which was suffering something like a discharge, touched it, and it was healed.[9]

3. Therefore, brothers, I would say this, I *do* say this; this, if I could, I would not be silent about: Let there be in you some works at one moment and others at another moment, in keeping with the time, in keeping with the hours, in keeping with the days. Is there always to be speaking? Is there always to be silence? Is there always to be feeding the body? Is there always to be fasting? Is there always to be giving bread to the needy? Is there always to be clothing the naked? Is there always to be

---

4. See Acts 9:1-30.
5. The allusion is to the Old Testament Saul who persecuted David. See 1 S 19:8ff.
6. See Acts 13:9.
7. "Little": *modicum.*
8. "A little later": *paulo post;* "after a little while": *post modicum.*
9. See Mt 9:20-22.

visiting the sick? Is there always to be promoting concord among the discordant? Is there always to be burying the dead? One time there is this, another time that. These things start and cease. But that general[10] neither starts nor should he cease. Let the charity that is within not be interrupted; let the duties of charity be carried out in accordance with the time. As it is written, then, *let brotherly charity abide* (Heb 13:1).

4. But perhaps some of you are wondering why, ever since we have been preaching to you on this epistle of the blessed John, he hasn't emphasized anything except brotherly charity. *He who loves his brother* (2:10), he says, and, *The commandment has been given to us to love one another* (3:23).[11] He mentioned brotherly charity incessantly, but the charity of God—that is, that whereby we must love God—he was not so incessant in mentioning, yet he wasn't entirely silent about it. But of the love of one's enemy he was utterly silent throughout almost all of that epistle. Although he preaches to us forcefully and commends charity, he doesn't tell us to love our enemies, but he does tell us to love our brothers. When the gospel was read a short while ago, however, we heard: *For if you love those who love you, what reward will you have? Do not the publicans also do this?* (Mt 5:46) Why is it, then, that the apostle John, with a view to a certain perfection, commends brotherly love to us as something great, whereas the Lord says that it isn't enough for us to love our brothers but that we must extend that love as far as our enemies? He who goes as far as his enemies doesn't pass over his brothers. Like fire, it first seizes upon the things that are nearby and in that way stretches out to what is more distant. Your brother is closer to you than anyone else that I can think of. On the other hand, he whom you didn't know, yet who isn't your adversary, is nearer to you than the enemy who is also your adversary. Extend your love to those who are closest, but you shouldn't call that an extension. For you who love those who are near to you love yourself closely. Extend your love to those who are unknown to you, who haven't done anything bad to you. Go even

---

10. See above 1.
11. This is a much abbreviated form of 3:23.

beyond them; go as far as loving your enemies. This is certainly what the Lord commands. Why is he[12] silent about the love of one's enemy?

5. Every love,[13] whether that which is called fleshly, which isn't love but instead tends to be called *amor* (for the word *dilectio* generally tends to be referred to better things and to be understood in reference to better things)—regardless, every love, dearest brothers, in fact implies a certain benevolence toward those who are loved. For it isn't in this way that we should love, or in this way that we can love, or love (*amare*) (for this word was even used by the Lord when he said, *Peter, do you love* [*amas*] *me?* [Jn 21:17])[14]—we shouldn't love (*amare*) people in the same way that we hear gourmands say, "I love (*amo*) thrushes." Do you ask why? So that he may kill and eat them. And he says that he loves (*amare*) them, and he loves (*amat*) so that they may not exist; he loves (*amat*) them so that he may destroy them. And, whatever we love (*amamus*) to eat, we love (*amamus*) so that it may be consumed and we may be fed. Are human beings to be loved (*amandi*) as though they are to be consumed? But there is a certain friendship of benevolence, which we sometimes offer to those whom we love (*amamus*). What if there is nothing to offer? Benevolence alone is enough for the one who loves (*amanti*).

For we mustn't wish that there be unfortunates, so that we may be able to exercise the works of mercy. You give bread to the hungry, but it would be better if no one were hungry and you gave to no one. You clothe the naked. Would that all were clothed and there weren't this need! You bury the dead. Would that that life would finally come in which no one dies! You bring concord to those who are quarreling. Would that there would finally be that eternal peace of Jerusalem, where no one is in discord! For all of these are the duties of necessity. Take away the unfortunates and the works of mercy will cease. The works of mercy will cease; will the warmth of charity be extinguished? You love (*amas*) with

---

12. *Iste*—i.e., John.

13. In this section I have translated *dilectio* simply as "love" and have kept *amor* in Latin. When the verb *amare* is used, it appears in parentheses next to the translation "love"; when the verb *diligere* is used, it is translated as "love" without further notice.

14. Augustine cites the Latin as if it were the language that Jesus used, whereas in fact the gospel is written in Greek. Augustine quotes Jn 21:15-17 with the same intention in *The City of God* XIV,14.

more genuineness a well-off person to whom you have nothing to offer. That love (*amor*) will be purer and much more sincere. For, if you have made an offering to an unfortunate, perhaps you desire to extol yourself over against him, and you want him—who is the author of your good deed—to be subject to you. He was needy, you bestowed something. You seem greater, because you made the offering, than him to whom the offering was made. Choose to be equal, so that both of you may be under the one to whom nothing can be offered.

6. For this is how the proud soul has exceeded the measure and in a certain way been avaricious, because *avarice is the root of all evils* (1 Tm 6:10). And similarly it is said that *pride is the beginning of every sin* (Sir 10:15). And there are times when we ask how these two phrases harmonize with each other—*Avarice is the root of all evils* and *Pride is the beginning of every sin.* If *pride is the beginning of every sin,* pride *is the root of all evils. Avarice is,* indeed, *the root of all evils:* we have found that avarice also exists in pride, for man has exceeded the measure. What does it mean to be avaricious? To go beyond what is enough. By pride Adam fell. *Pride is the beginning of every sin,* it says. What about avarice? What more avaricious than he for whom God wasn't enough? Well then, brothers, we have read how man was made to the image and likeness of God.[15] And what did God say of him? *And let him have power over the fish of the sea and the birds of the sky and all the beasts that crawl upon the earth* (Gn 1:26). Did he say, "Let him have power over men"? *Let him have power,* he said. He gave an innate[16] power. Over what would he have power? *Over the fish of the sea, the birds of the sky, and all the crawling things that crawl upon the earth.* Why is this innate power of man in that? Because man has power from the fact that he has been made to the image of God. But where has he been made to the image of God?[17] In his understanding, in his mind, in the inner man, in that which understands the truth, distinguishes righteousness and unrigh-

---

15. See Gn 1:26.
16. "Innate": *naturalem.*
17. Although a few lines previously he had referred to man's having been made in both the image and the likeness of God, here Augustine discusses only the image, which in his view (as in that of many other patristic writers) implies the likeness. See Mary T. Clark, "Image Doctrine," in

teousness, knows by whom he was made, and is able to understand his
creator and to praise his creator. He who has prudence has this understanding. Hence, when through their evil desires many were weakening
the image of God in themselves and, by the perversity of their behavior,
were in some way extinguishing the very flame of understanding, scripture cried out to them: *Do not become like the horse and the mule, which
have no understanding* (Ps 32:9). That is to say: "I have placed you
ahead of the horse and the mule; I have made you to my image; I have
given you power over them. Why? Because wild animals don't have a
rational mind, but with your rational mind you grasp truth, you understand what is above you." Submit to him because he is above you, and
those whom you have been set over will be beneath you. But, because
through sin man abandoned him whom he should have been under, he is
subjected to those whom he should have been over.

7. Pay heed to what I say: God, man, beasts. Clearly God is above you,
the beasts are below you. Acknowledge him who is above you, so that
those who are beneath you may acknowledge you. Hence, when Daniel
had acknowledged that God was above him, the lions acknowledged that
he was above them.[18] If, however, you don't acknowledge him who is
above you, you disdain him who is superior and submit to what is inferior. How, then, was the pride of the Egyptians tamed? With frogs and
flies.[19] God could even have sent lions, but it is someone great who must
be frightened by a lion. The prouder they were, the more it was by
contemptible and lowly things that their wicked neck was brought down.
But the lions acknowledged Daniel because he was subject to God.

What? Weren't the martyrs, who fought with the beasts and were
ravaged by the bites of wild animals, under God? And weren't the three
men servants of God, and weren't the Maccabees servants of God? The
fire acknowledged that the three men were servants of God; the fire

---

Augustine through the Ages 440-442. The second half of *The Trinity* is Augustine's greatest
contribution to the theology of the divine image.
18. See Dn 6:22.
19. See Ex 7:26-8:11; 8:16-28.

didn't burn them, nor did it destroy their garments.[20] And didn't it recognize the Maccabees? It recognized the Maccabees; brothers, it recognized them as well. But there was need of a certain scourge, by the permission of the Lord, who said in scripture, *He scourges every son whom he accepts* (Heb 12:6). For do you think, brothers, that the iron would have pierced the Lord's breast if he himself hadn't permitted it, or that he would have clung to the wood if he himself hadn't wanted it? Did his creature not acknowledge him? Or was he offering an example of patience to his believers? And so God liberated some visibly, and some he didn't liberate visibly, yet he liberated all spiritually, and he abandoned no one spiritually. He seemed to have abandoned some visibly, and some he seemed to have snatched away. Some he snatched away lest you think that he couldn't snatch them away. He gave proof that he can, so that, when he doesn't do it, you may understand his more obscure will and not suspect a difficulty. And then, brothers? When we have escaped all the snares of mortality, when the times of temptation have passed, when this world's stream has run its course and we have received the first robe,[21] that immortality which we lost by sinning, when this corruptible has put on incorruption—that is, when the flesh has put on incorruption—and this mortal has put on immortality,[22] every creature shall acknowledge the now-perfected children of God, when there is no need to be tempted or to be scourged; all creatures shall be subjected to us if here we have been subjected to God.

8. A Christian must live in such a way as not to exalt himself over other people. For God has given you an existence above that of the beasts—that is, a better existence than that of the beasts. This you have as something innate: you will always be better than the beasts. If you wish to be better than another human being, you will be envious of him when you see that he is your equal. You must want all human beings to be equal to you, and, if you have surpassed anyone in prudence, you must desire

---

20. See Dn 3:50.
21. "First robe": *stolam primam*. See the Latin of Lk 15:22, where it has the sense of the best robe or the robe of honor. Rettig notes the use of this term in *The Literal Meaning of Genesis* VI,20,31 and VI,27,38; in the former place it refers to the immortality that Adam lost by sinning and in the latter to either the justice or the immortality that he lost.
22. See 1 Cor 15:53.

that he himself also be prudent. As long as he is slow, he learns from you; as long as he is uninstructed, he needs you; and it looks as though you are the teacher and he the learner. You, then, are superior, because you are the teacher; he is inferior, because he is learning. Unless you wish him to be your equal, you want to have him always as a learner. But if you want to have him always as a learner, you will be an envious teacher. If you are an envious teacher, how will you be a teacher? I beg you, don't teach him your own envy. Listen to the Apostle as he speaks from the depths of charity: *I would want all men to be like myself* (1 Cor 7:7). How did he want all to be equal? He was superior to all because, out of charity, he wished all to be equal. That is how man exceeded the measure: he wanted to be more avaricious, so that he who was made above the beasts would be above men, and that is pride.

9. And see how many works pride does.[23] Give thought to how similar to and as though on a par with charity it makes them. Charity feeds the hungry man; pride also feeds him. Charity does it so that God may be praised, pride so that it itself may be praised. Charity clothes the naked man; pride also clothes him. Charity fasts; pride also fasts. Charity buries the dead; pride also buries them. Pride, directing its horses, as it were, carries out in contrary fashion all the good works that charity wants to do and does do. But charity is within; it removes the place of the badly-driven pride—not badly driving but badly-driven. Woe to the man whose chariot is pride, for it will surely be wrecked.

But who knows whether it isn't pride that carries out good deeds? Who sees? Where is this? We see the works. Mercy feeds; pride also feeds. Mercy welcomes the stranger; pride also welcomes the stranger. Mercy intervenes on behalf of the poor man; pride also intervenes. What does this mean? We make no distinction in the works. I dare to say something, but not I. Paul said it: Charity dies—that is, the person who has charity confesses the name of Christ and undergoes martyrdom. Pride also confesses; it also undergoes martyrdom. The one has charity; the other doesn't have charity. But let him who doesn't have charity hear from the Apostle: *If I distribute everything that I have to the poor, and if I hand*

---

23. This section recalls VII,7-8.

over my body to be burned, but do not have charity, it is of no benefit to me (1 Cor 13:3). Hence the divine scripture inwardly beckons us away from the boastfulness of this appearance outwardly, and from that surface which boasts in the presence of men it beckons us to what is within. Return to your conscience; question it. Pay attention not to what blossoms without but to what root is in the earth. Is cupidity rooted there? There can be the appearance of good deeds, but good works cannot be there. Is charity rooted there? Be secure: nothing wicked can grow. The proud man flatters; love is violent. The one clothes; the other beats. For the one clothes in order to please men; the other beats so that discipline may correct. The blows of charity are more acceptable than the alms of pride. Go within, then, brothers, and in everything, whatever you may do, glimpse God as your witness. See, if he sees, with what mind you act. If your heart doesn't accuse you of acting out of pride, it is well: be secure. But don't fear that, when you act well, someone else may not see you. Fear lest you act so that you may be praised, for another person ought to see so that God may be praised. For, if you hide from the eyes of man, you are hiding from the imitation of man and withdrawing praise from God. There are two to whom you give alms: two are hungry—one for bread and the other for justice. Between these two hungry persons, because it is said, *Blessed are those who hunger and thirst for justice, for they shall be filled* (Mt 5:6)—between these two hungry persons, you have been made a doer of good. If charity works in the case of one, it would have mercy on both, it wants to help both. For one seeks something to eat; the other seeks something to imitate. You feed the one; you offer[24] yourself to the other. To both you have given alms: the former you have made grateful for the hunger that you slew; the latter you have made the imitator of the example that you proposed.

10. Be merciful, then, in the way that merciful people are, because by also loving your enemies you are loving your brothers. Don't think that John commanded nothing with respect to the love of one's enemy, because he wasn't silent about brotherly charity. You love your

---

24. Reading *praebes* ("you offer"), as attested by several manuscripts, rather than *praebe* ("offer"), also attested by several manuscripts.

brothers. How, you say, do we love our brothers? I ask why you should love your enemy. Why do you love him? So that he may be well in this life? What if that isn't good for him? So that he may be rich? What if he is blinded by those very riches? So that he may marry a wife? What if he endures a bitter life as a result? So that he may have children? What if they turn out to be wicked? The things, then, that you seem to wish for your enemy, because you love him, are uncertain. They are uncertain: wish [instead] for him that he may have eternal life along with you; wish for him that he may be your brother. If this is what you wish, that by loving your enemy he may be your brother, you are loving your brother when you love him. For you aren't loving in him what is but what you want to be.

Unless I am mistaken, I had at some point said to Your Charity: Set before your eyes the trunk of a tree.[25] A very skilled craftsman has seen the unhewn wood, cut from the forest, and has fallen in love[26] with it. I don't know what he wants to make of it. For he hasn't loved it so that it will always remain as it is. Thanks to his craftsmanship he has seen what it *will be*—not, thanks to his love, what it *is*. And he has loved what he is going to make of it, not what it is. This is also the way that God has loved us sinners. We say that God loved sinners, for he said, *The healthy do not need a physician, but those who are ill* (Mt 9:12). Did he love sinners so that we would remain sinners? The creator has looked upon us as though we were wood from the forest, and he has pictured the structure that he is going to make of it, not the forest as it was. So too you regard your enemy—adversarial, furious, biting in his speech, provoking in his slander, railing in his hatred. You are attentive to the fact that he is a human being. You see all those things that are adverse, that were done by a human being, and you see in him that he was made by God. On the one hand, that he was made a man means that he was made by God. On the other, that he hates you is something that *he* has done; that he is envious is something that *he* has done. And what do you say in your soul? "Lord, be gracious to him, forgive him his sins. Strike him with terror, change

---

25. Augustine did not present this image in these homilies.
26. "Fallen in love": *adamavit*. Augustine chooses a strong word here.

him." You don't love what is in him but what you want him to be. When you love your enemy, therefore, you are loving your brother.

Hence perfect love is love of one's enemy, and this perfect love consists in brotherly love. And no one should say that the apostle John has taught us anything less and that the Lord Christ has taught us more. John taught us to love our brothers; Christ taught us even to love our enemies.[27] Pay heed to why Christ taught you to love your enemies. So that they would always remain enemies? If Christ taught you this so that they would remain enemies, you are hating and not loving them. Pay heed to how he himself loved—that is, that he didn't want them to remain his persecutors. He said, *Father, forgive them, because they do not know what they are doing* (Lk 23:34). He wanted them to be forgiven, he wanted them to be changed. Those whom he wanted to be changed he deigned to make brothers from enemies, and he truly made them thus. He was killed, he was buried, he rose, he ascended into heaven, he sent the Holy Spirit to his disciples; they began to preach his name with confidence; they performed miracles in the name of the one who had been crucified and killed. Those killers of the Lord saw, and those who in their fury poured out his blood drank it in their belief.[28]

11. I have said these things, brothers, and done so at some length, yet, because this charity had to be commended quite emphatically to Your Charity, this, then, was how it had to be commended. For if there is no charity in you, we have said nothing. But, if it is in you, it is as though we have added oil to flame. And, in him in whom it was not, perhaps it has been set ablaze by these words. In one person what was there has grown; in another what wasn't there has begun. We have said these things so that you may not be sluggish in loving your enemies. Is someone furious at you? He is furious, you pray; he hates, you have mercy. It is his soul's fever that hates you; he will be healed, and he will be grateful to you. How do physicians love the sick? *Do* they love the sick? If they love them as sick persons, they want them always to be sick. They love the sick not so that they may remain sick but so that they may become well

27. See Mt 5:44.
28. The allusion is to the cup of the eucharist. See also I,9.

from having been sick. And how much do they frequently endure from those who are delirious! How much abusive language! Frequently they are even struck. He goes after the fever and forgives the person.[29] And what shall I say, brothers—that he loves his enemy? In fact he hates his enemy, which is the illness. That is the very thing that he hates, and he loves the person by whom he is being struck. He hates the fever. For by what is he being struck? By the illness, by the sickness, by the fever. He removes what is opposed to him so that that may remain for which he may give thanks. It is the same with you. If your enemy hates you, and he hates you unjustly, you should know that he hates you because the cupidity of the world reigns in him. If you also hate him, you are returning evil for evil. What makes a person return evil for evil? I used to sorrow over one sick person who hated you. Now I bewail two, if you also hate him. But he is after your property. He takes from you something or other that you have on earth, and therefore you hate him, because he has created hardships for you on earth. Don't endure the hardships; go off to heaven above. You will have your heart in a spacious place, so that you may endure no hardships in the hope of eternal life.[30] Pay heed to what he is taking away from you. He wouldn't take those things away unless he who *scourges every son whom he accepts* permitted it. Your enemy himself is in a certain way the sword of God by which you are healed. If God knows that it is beneficial for you that he plunder you, he permits him; if he knows that it is beneficial for you that he flog you, he permits him, so that you are beaten. It is thanks to him that he cures you; desire that he be healed.

12. *No one has ever seen God* (4:12). See, beloved: *If we love one another, God will abide in us, and his love will be perfected in us* (4:12). Begin to love, to be made perfect. Have you begun to love? God has begun to dwell in you. Love him who has begun to dwell in you, so that by dwelling in you more perfectly he may make you perfect. *We know*

---

29. Here Augustine has switched from the plural to the singular, which suggests a certain extemporaneous quality in his speaking.
30. "Spacious place": *latitudo*; "hardships": *angustias*. The root *angust* means "narrow," hence "hard" or "difficult." The contrast between the narrow and the spacious is lost in the English translation.

that we abide in him, and he in us, because he has given us of his Spirit (4:13). Good! Thanks be to God! We know that he dwells in us. And how do we know this very thing, that we have known that he dwells in us? Because John himself said, *Because he has given us of his Spirit.* How do we know that *he has given us of his Spirit*? How do *you* know this very thing, that he has given *you* of his Spirit? Ask your heart. If it is filled with charity, you have God's Spirit. How do we know that that is how you know that God's Spirit dwells in you? Ask the apostle Paul: *Because the charity of God has been poured out in our hearts through the Holy Spirit, who has been given to us* (Rom 5:5).

13. *And we have seen, and we are witnesses, that the Father sent his Son as the savior of the world* (4:14). Be at ease, you who are sick. So great a physician has come, and do you despair? The illnesses were great, the wounds were incurable, the sickness was hopeless. You are aware of the greatness of the evil, and are you unaware of the physician's omnipotence? You are desperate, but he is omnipotent. His witnesses are those who were first healed and who proclaim the physician. And yet even they themselves were healed more in hope than in reality. For this is what the Apostle says: *For by hope we have been saved* (Rom 8:24). We begin to be saved, then, in faith, but our salvation will be made perfect when this corruptible puts on incorruption and this mortal puts on immortality.[31] This hope isn't yet reality. But he who rejoices in hope[32] will also seize upon the reality. He who doesn't have hope, however, will be unable to arrive at the reality.

14. *Whoever confesses that Jesus is the Son of God, God abides in him and he in God* (4:15). Now let us say this briefly: whoever confesses not in word but in deed, not in speech but in life. For many confess it in words but deny it by their deeds. *And we have known and have believed what love God has in us* (4:16). And, once again, how have you known? *God is love* (4:16). He already said that previously; see, he says it again. Love could be commended to you no more fully than by referring to it as God.

---

31. See 1 Cor 15:53.51.
32. See Rom 12:12.

Perhaps you had disdained God's gift. And do you disdain God? *God is love, and he who abides in love abides in God, and God abides in him* (4:16). The one who contains and the one who is contained dwell mutually in each other. You dwell in God, but in such a way that you are contained; God dwells in you, but in such a way that he contains you, lest you be diminished. Don't perhaps think that you have become God's dwelling in the same way that your dwelling carries your flesh. If the dwelling in which you are is removed, you are diminished; but if you remove yourself, God isn't diminished. He is complete when you depart from him and complete when you return to him. You are healed; you won't bestow anything on him. You are cleansed, you are refreshed, you are corrected. He is medicine for the one who is unwell, he is a rule for the wayward, he is a light for the one in darkness, he is a dwelling for the abandoned. All things, then, are given to you. See that you don't think that anything is being given to God when you come to him, not even your own servitude. Will God not have slaves, then, if you are unwilling and if everyone is unwilling? God has no need of slaves, but the slaves do of God. Hence the psalm says, *I said to the Lord, You are my God* (Ps 16:2).[33] He is the true Lord. And what does it say? *Because you have no need of my goods* (Ps 16:2). You need the good of your own slave. Your slave needs your good, so that you may feed him, and you also need the good of your slave, so that he may help you. You cannot draw water for yourself, you cannot cook for yourself, you cannot run before your horse for yourself, you cannot care for your beast of burden. You see that you are in need of your slave's good, you are in need of his obedience. You are no true lord, then, when you are in need of an inferior. He is the true Lord who seeks nothing from us. And woe to us if we don't seek him. He seeks nothing from us, and he sought us when we weren't seeking him. A single sheep had wandered off. He found him and, rejoicing,

---

33. The Latin *dominus*, translated here as "Lord," also means "master," which is the more usual term for someone who owns slaves.

brought him back on his shoulders.[34] And was the sheep necessary to the shepherd, or wasn't rather the shepherd necessary to the sheep?

The more eagerly I speak of charity, the less I want this epistle to come to an end. None is more ardent in commending charity. Nothing is preached to you more sweetly, nothing is imbibed more healthfully—but only if by living well you strengthen the gift of God in yourselves. Don't be ungrateful regarding that great grace of him who, although he had an only Son, didn't want him to be alone, but, so that he would have brothers, adopted them, so that with him they would possess eternal life.

---

34. See Lk 15:4-5.

Ninth Homily

1. Your Charity recalls that the final part of the epistle of the apostle John remains to be discussed by us and to be explained to you, as much as the Lord allows. We are mindful, then, of this debt, but you must be mindful of exacting it. The same charity, indeed, which in this epistle is especially and almost solely commended, makes us the most trustworthy debtors and you the sweetest creditors. I said "the sweetest creditors" because, where there is no charity, the creditor is bitter. But, where there is charity, the creditor is sweet, and, as far as the debtor is concerned, even if he bears some burden, charity makes that same burden almost nothing and light. Don't we see even in dumb and irrational animals, where charity isn't spiritual but rather fleshly and innate,[1] that milk is nonetheless exacted by the young from their mother's breasts with great affection? And, although the suckling exerts pressure on her breasts, still it is better for the mother than if he doesn't suck or exact what is owed by charity. We often see cows' breasts being butted even by more or less fully grown calves and the mothers' bodies being nearly lifted up by that force, and yet they are not kicked away. On the contrary, if a young one is missing that should be sucking, he is called to the breasts with bellowing. If, then, there is in us that spiritual charity of which the Apostle says, *I became a little child in your midst, like a nurse caring for her children* (1 Thes 2:7), then we love you when you make an exaction. We don't love the sluggish, because we are anxious about those who are unmotivated.

But certain customary readings for the feast days—which had to be read and preached on—have intervened, so that we laid aside the text of

---

1. "Innate": *naturalis*. See Sermon 349,2 on the charity that animals have for their young, as well as on other forms of charity that would qualify as not "spiritual but rather fleshly and innate" (such as that exercised by "pagans, Jews and heretics").

this epistle.[2] Now let us return, then, to the sequence that was interrupted, and may Your Holiness receive attentively what remains.

I don't know whether charity could be commended to us more magnificently than by the words *God is charity* (4:8). The praise is brief and the praise is great—brief in words and great in intellectual depth.[3] How quickly it is said that *God is love!*[4] And this is brief. If you should number it, it is one thing. If you should weigh it, how much it is! *God is love, and he who abides in love*, it says, *abides in God, and God abides in him* (4:16). Let God be your dwelling, and let your dwelling be God's. Abide in God, and let God abide in you. God abides in you so that he may contain you; you abide in God lest you fall, because that is how the Apostle speaks of charity: *Charity never falls* (1 Cor 13:8). How does he whom God contains fall?

2. *This is how love is perfected in us, that we have confidence regarding the day of judgment,*[5] *because, as he is, so also are we in this world* (4:17). He tells how each person may examine himself as to how much progress charity has made in him, or rather as to how much he has made progress in charity. For, if *God is charity*, God neither progresses nor regresses. That is how charity is said to progress in you—that you progress in it. Ask, then, how much you have progressed in charity, and let your heart respond as to what it is, so that you may know the extent of your progress.

---

2. These feast days (*diebus festis*) were almost certainly part of the Easter cycle, and it is clear that at this point the homilies have extended beyond Easter Week. This homily and the final one may have even been delivered after the feast of the Ascension, forty days after Easter, inasmuch as the Ascension is mentioned in X,3.9. See Rettig 246, note 1. But the hiatus between Easter Week and the Ascension seems much longer than is suggested by Augustine's cursory explanation for laying aside the epistle.

3. "In intellectual depth": *in intellectu.*

4. Whereas in the previous citation from the epistle the word *caritas* was used, now *dilectio* is used. Augustine repeats *caritas* in 2 below.

5. *That we have confidence regarding the day of judgment: ut fiduciam habeamus in die iudicii.* Brown 528 argues that the Greek text demands that the translation be *on the day of judgment,* although other scholars whom he mentions say that the better rendering is along the lines of the one used here. In any case, from what follows it seems clear that Augustine himself understands the confidence in question as that which one would have in respect to a future event (*looking forward to* judgment day) rather than as that which one would have while the future event was occurring (*on* judgment day). That calls for *regarding* rather than *on.*

For he promised to show us how we may know him, and he said, *This is how love is perfected in us.* I ask how. *That we have confidence regarding the day of judgment.* Whoever has confidence regarding the day of judgment, in him has charity been perfected. What does it mean to have confidence regarding the day of judgment? Not to fear lest the day of judgment come. There are persons who don't believe in the day of judgment; they can't have confidence regarding a day which they don't believe will come. Let us leave them aside. God may arouse them so that they may live, but what is there for us to say about the dead? They don't believe in the future day of judgment, and they neither fear nor desire what they don't believe in. Someone has begun to believe in the day of judgment; if he has begun to believe, he has also begun to fear. But, because he still fears, he doesn't yet have confidence regarding the day of judgment; there is as yet no perfect charity in him. Is he nonetheless to be despaired of? In the person in whom you see the beginning, why do you despair of the end? You ask what beginning I see. Fear itself. Listen to scripture: *The fear of the Lord is the beginning of wisdom* (Sir 1:16). He has begun, then, to fear the day of judgment. Let him amend himself by fearing. Let him be watchful against his enemies—that is, against his sins. Let him begin to renew his life within and to mortify his members that are on earth, as the Apostle says, *Mortify your members that are on earth* (Col 3:5). He refers to the spiritual qualities of wickedness as *members on earth*, for he continues and explains: *Avarice, uncleanness* (Col 3:5), and the other things that follow there. The heavenly members rise up and are fortified, however, to the degree that he who has begun to fear the day of judgment mortifies his members on earth. Now the heavenly members are all good works. Once the heavenly members have risen up, he begins to desire what he once feared. For he used to fear that Christ would come and find him evil and condemn him. He desires that he come, because he will find him good and crown him. Since the chaste soul, which desires the bridegroom's embraces, has now begun to desire Christ's coming, she becomes a virgin through faith, hope and charity. Now she has confidence regarding the day of judgment. She doesn't struggle against herself when she prays and says, *Your kingdom come*

(Mt 6:10). For he who fears that God's kingdom will come fears that his prayer may be answered. How does one pray who fears that his prayer may be answered? But he who prays with the confidence of charity wishes for him to come now. Of this same desire someone said in a psalm: *And you, Lord, how long? Turn, Lord, and rescue my soul.* (Ps 6:3-4) He groans at his delay. For there are persons who die with patience, but there are some who are perfect who live with patience.

What did I mean? He who still desires this life when the day of death comes to him endures death patiently. He struggles against himself to follow God's will, and in his mind he inclines toward what God chooses and not what his human will chooses. And from his yearning for the present life there arises the struggle with death, and he exercises patience and fortitude so that he may die with equanimity. That person dies patiently. But he who desires, as the Apostle says, *to be dissolved and to be with Christ* (Phil 1:23) doesn't die patiently; instead he lives patiently and dies in delight. See how patiently the Apostle lives—that is, not loving life here but enduring it with patience. *To be dissolved and to be with Christ is by far the best thing, but to remain in the flesh is necessary for your sake* (Phil 1:23-24). Therefore, brothers, make an effort, come to an agreement within yourselves, so that you may desire the day of judgment. There is no proof that your charity is perfect until that day has begun to be desired. But he who has confidence regarding it is the one who desires it, and he whose conscience, in perfect and sincere charity, isn't afraid is the one who has confidence regarding it.

3. *This is how his love is perfected in us, that we have confidence regarding the day of judgment.* Why shall we have confidence? *Because, just as he is, so also are we in this world.* You have heard the cause of our confidence. *Because, just as he is,* he says, *so also are we in this world.* Doesn't he seem to have said something impossible? For can a human being be just as God is?

I have already explained to you that "just as" doesn't always refer to equality but refers to a certain likeness.[6] For how do you say, "A statue has ears just as I do"? Is that really how it is? But still you say "just as." If,

---

6. See IV,9.

then, we have been made to the image of God, why aren't we just as God is? [We are—yet] not in terms of equality but according to our measure. Where, then, is confidence given to us regarding the day of judgment? Because, just as he is, so also are we in this world. We must refer this to charity itself and understand what has been said. The Lord says in the gospel, *If you love those who love you, what reward will you have? Do not the publicans also do this?* (Mt 5:46) What does he want from us, then? *But I tell you, Love your enemies, and pray for those who persecute you* (Mt 5:44). If, then, he commands us to love our enemies, from whom does he give us an example? From God himself, for he says, *That you may be sons of your Father who is in heaven* (Mt 5:45). How does God do this? He loves his enemies, *who makes his sun rise on the good and the bad and his rain fall on the righteous and the unrighteous* (Mt 5:45). If God summons us to this perfection, then, so that we may love our enemies just as he himself also loved them, we have confidence regarding the day of judgment because, *just as he is, so also are we in this world.* For, just as he loves his enemies by making his sun rise on the good and the bad and by raining on the righteous and the unrighteous, so also we, inasmuch as we cannot provide sun and rain for our enemies, offer them our tears when we pray for them.

4. Now then, see what he says about this very confidence. How is perfect charity understood? *There is no fear in charity* (4:18). What is there for us to say, then, about him who has begun to fear the day of judgment? If the charity in him were perfect, he wouldn't fear it. For perfect charity would bring about perfect righteousness, and he would have no reason to fear it. Indeed, he would have a reason to desire that wickedness would pass away and the reign of God would come. Hence *there is no fear in charity.* But in what charity? Not when it is beginning. In what, then? *But,* he says, *perfect charity casts out fear* (4:18). Let fear begin, then, *because the fear of the Lord is the beginning of wisdom.* Fear as it were prepares a place for charity. But when charity has begun to take up residence, the fear that had prepared a place for it is driven out. The former increases to the extent that the latter decreases, and the former becomes more interior to the extent that fear is driven out. The greater the

charity, the less the fear; the less the charity, the greater the fear. But if there is no fear, there is no way that charity may come in. For example, we see that thread is inserted by a needle when something is being sewn: the needle goes in first, but, unless it comes out, the thread doesn't follow. Similarly, fear occupies the mind first, but fear doesn't remain there, because it has entered in order to introduce charity. Once security has been established in the soul, what joy there is for us both in this and in the future world! And in this world who will harm us if we are filled with charity? See how the Apostle exults with regard to this very charity. *Who*, he says, *will separate us from the charity of Christ? Tribulation, or difficulty, or persecution, or hunger, or nakedness, or danger, or the sword?* (Rom 8:35) And Peter says, *And who can harm you if you are followers of the good?* (1 Pt 3:13)

There is no fear in love, but perfect love casts out fear,[7] *because fear has torment*[8] (4:18). As long as righteousness hasn't been accomplished, the conscience of sinners tortures their heart. There is something there that would scratch and that would prick. What does it say in a psalm, then, about that very perfection of righteousness? *You turned my mourning into joy for me. You cut away my sackcloth and girded me with gladness, so that my glory might sing to you, and so that I would not be pricked.* (Ps 30:11-12) What does this mean, *so that I would not be pricked*? There is nothing that would goad my conscience. Fear goads, but don't fear. Let charity enter in, which heals what fear wounds. The fear of God wounds in the same way as a physician's scalpel: it removes the festering and seems as it were to enlarge the wound. See, when there was festering in the body the wound was smaller but dangerous. The physician's scalpel appears: that wound used to pain less than it pains now that it is being cut. While being treated it pains more than if it weren't being treated. But when medicine is applied it is still more painful, so that it may never pain once health has been restored. Let fear occupy your heart, then, so that it may bring in charity; let the scab give

---

7. When previously citing this passage, Augustine had used the term "charity" (*caritas*), but here he uses "love" (*dilectio*). In 5 below he reverts to "charity."

8. Augustine's Latin text had *tormentum* rather than the more usual *poenam* ("punishment") or its equivalent.

way to the physician's scalpel. Such is the physician that scabs don't even appear; you only need to place yourself under his hand. For, if you are without fear, you won't be able to be made righteous. These are the words that were spoken in scripture: *For he who is without fear will not be able to be made righteous* (Sir 1:28). Fear, then, must be the first to enter in, through which charity may come. Fear is the medicine, charity is health. *But he who fears is not perfect in love* (4:18). Why? *Because fear has torment*, just as a physician's cutting has torment.

5. But there are other passages that seem to contradict this, if there is no one to understand them. For it is said in a certain place in a psalm, *The fear of the Lord is chaste, abiding forever* (Ps 19:9). [The psalmist] refers us to a certain eternal but chaste fear. But if he refers us to an eternal fear, doesn't the epistle perhaps contradict him, which says, *There is no fear in charity, but perfect charity casts out fear?*

Let us question both utterances of God. There is one Spirit even if there are two codexes, even if there are two mouths, even if there are two tongues. For the latter was said by John and the former was said by David,[9] but don't think that the Spirit is something else. If one breath blows into two pipes, can't one Spirit fill two hearts and set two tongues in motion?[10] But if two pipes harmonize when they are filled with one spirit—that is, with one breath—can two tongues be disharmonious when they are filled with the Spirit of God? There is, then, a certain harmony, there is a certain concord, but it seeks a listener. See, the Spirit of God blew into and filled two hearts and two mouths, and he moved two tongues, and we heard in one tongue: *There is no fear in charity, but perfect charity casts out fear*; in another we heard: *The fear of the Lord is chaste, abiding forever.* What does this mean? Is it as though they are disharmonious? No: open wide your ears, listen to the melody. Not without reason did he add *chaste* in one place and not add it in the other, inasmuch as there is one fear that is called chaste, while there is another that isn't called chaste. Let us distinguish between these two fears and

9. According to the understanding of the early Church, David was the author of all the psalms.
10. "Breath": *flatus*; "Spirit": *spiritus*. Here Augustine makes a distinction, although the words can be used synonymously, but later in this homily, in section 9, he relies exclusively on *spiritus* when developing the metaphor of the pipes.

understand the harmony of the pipes. How do we understand, or how do we distinguish? Let Your Charity be attentive. There are people who fear the Lord so that they may not be sent to Gehenna, so that they may not perchance burn with the devil in eternal fire. This is the fear that introduces charity, but it arrives in this way so that it may leave. For if you still fear God on account of punishment, you don't yet love him whom you fear in that way. You aren't desiring good things but being fearful of evil things. But, by reason of the fact that you are fearful of evil things, you are correcting yourself and are beginning to desire good things. When you have begun to desire good things, there will be chaste fear in you. What is a chaste fear? That you may lose those good things themselves. Pay heed: it is one thing to fear God so that he may not send you to Gehenna with the devil; it is another to fear God so that he may not depart from you. The fear whereby you fear that you may be sent to Gehenna with the devil isn't yet chaste, for it doesn't come from the love of God but from the fear of punishment, but, when you fear God so that his presence may not leave you, you are embracing him, you are desiring to enjoy him.

6. The distinction between these two fears—the one which charity casts out and the other which remains chaste forever—can't be better explained than by imagining two married women. One of them you may picture as wanting to commit adultery and to take pleasure in wickedness but fearing that she may be condemned by her husband. She fears her husband, but she fears her husband because she still loves wickedness. To her the presence of her husband isn't pleasant but burdensome, and, if perhaps she is living wickedly, she fears her husband because he may come. Such are those who fear that the day of judgment will come. Picture another woman who loves her husband, who owes him chaste embraces, who does not sully herself with any adulterous uncleanness; she longs for her husband's presence. And how are these two fears distinguished? The one fears, and the other fears as well. Ask them. They give a single answer to you. Ask the one: "Do you fear your husband?" She replies, "I fear him." Ask the other also if she fears her husband. She replies, "I fear him." There is a single voice but a different state of mind.

Now, then, they are asked: "Why?" The one says, "I fear my husband because he may come." The other says, "I fear my husband because he may leave." The one says, "I fear that I may be condemned." The other says, "I fear that I may be left." Transpose this into the souls of Christians and you find the fear that charity casts out and another fear that is chaste and that abides forever.

7. Let us speak first, then, to those who fear God in the same way as does that woman whom wickedness delights, for she fears her husband because he may condemn her. Let us speak first to persons of that sort. O soul that fears God in that way, because God may condemn you, as the woman fears whom wickedness delights (she fears her husband because she may be condemned by her husband), just as that woman displeases you, so you also be displeasing to yourself. If perhaps you have a wife, do you want your wife to fear you because she may be condemned by you, so that wickedness may delight her but she may be curbed by the weight of fearing you and not by the condemnation of her wickedness? You want her to be chaste so that she may love you, not so that she may fear you. Show yourself to God as the sort of person that you want to have as your wife. And if you don't yet have one and want to have one, that is the kind that you want to have. And what are we saying, brothers? The woman who fears her husband because she may be condemned by her husband perhaps doesn't commit adultery, because her husband may somehow become aware of it and may remove from her this temporal light.[11] But her husband can also be deceived, for he is a human being, just as she is, who can be deceived. She fears him, beyond whose sight she can be. Don't you always fear the face of your husband over you? *But the face of the Lord is over those who do evil* (Ps 34:16). She longs for her husband's absence, and perhaps she is incited by the pleasure of adultery, and yet she says to herself, "I won't do it. He is absent, to be sure, but it is very unlikely that this wouldn't come to him in some way or other." She restrains herself because this may come to her husband, who is also capable of not knowing, who is also capable of being deceived, who is also capable of suspecting that even the bad is good, who is also capable

---

11. I.e., he may kill her.

of suspecting that she who is an adulteress is chaste. Don't you fear the eyes of him whom no one can deceive? Don't you fear the presence of him who can't be turned away from you? Beseech God to look upon you and to turn his face away from your sins: *Turn your face away from my sins* (Ps 51:9). But how do you merit that he turn his face away from your sins if you don't turn your own face away from your sins? For this is the very word that is spoken in the psalm: *Because I acknowledge my wickedness, and my sin is always before me* (Ps 51:3). You acknowledge, and he forgives.

8. We have addressed her who still has fear that doesn't abide forever but that charity excludes and casts out. Let us also address her who now has chaste fear, abiding forever. Do we think that we have found her, so that we may address her? Do you think that she is in this congregation? Do you think that she is in this hall? Do you think that she is on this earth? She cannot but be, yet she is hidden. It is winter, and the greenness is within, in the root. Perhaps we have found her ears. But, wherever that soul is, would that I would find her, and she wouldn't offer her ears to me but I would offer my ears to her! She would teach me something, rather than learning from me. A certain holy soul, ardent, and desirous of God's kingdom: it isn't I who address her but God himself, and this is how she is consoled as she lives patiently on this earth: "You want me to come now, and I know that you want me to come now. I know how you are, that you are awaiting my coming in peace. I know that this is irksome for you, but continue to wait and to endure. I am coming, and I am coming quickly."[12] But, for the one who loves, this is a delay. Listen to her singing like the lily in the midst of thorns. Listen to her sighing and saying: *I shall sing and I shall understand on the unsullied way. When will you come to me?* (Ps 101:1-2) But she rightly doesn't fear on an unsullied way, because *perfect charity casts out fear.* And, when she comes to his embrace, she fears, but in peace. What does she fear? She will be on her guard, and she will keep herself from all her wickedness, lest she sin again—not lest she be cast into the fire but lest she be left by him. And what will there be in her? A chaste fear, abiding forever.

---

12. See Rev 22:20.

We have heard the two pipes sounding together. The one speaks of fear and the other speaks of fear, but the one of a fear whereby the soul fears that she may be condemned, the other of a fear whereby the soul fears that she may be left. That is the fear which charity excludes; it is the fear that abides forever.

9. *Let us love, because he loved us first* (4:19). For how would we love if he had not loved us first? By his love we were made his friends, but he loved us as enemies so that we would become his friends. He loved us first and bestowed on us the means of loving him. What does an ugly man with a twisted face do if he loves a beautiful woman? Or what does an ugly and twisted and swarthy woman do if she loves a beautiful man? Will she be able, by loving, to be beautiful? And will he be able, by loving, to be handsome? He loves a beautiful woman, and, when he looks at himself in a mirror, he is ashamed to raise his face to that beautiful one of his[13] whom he loves. What will he do to be beautiful? Does he wait for beauty to come to him? In fact old age is added by waiting, and it makes him more unattractive. There is nothing for him to do, then; there is no way for you to advise him, except that he should restrain himself and not dare to love on an unequal basis. Or, if perhaps he is in love and wishes to take her as his wife, let him love the chastity that is in her, not the appearance of the flesh. But our soul, my brothers, is loathsome through wickedness; by loving God it is made beautiful. What sort of love is it that makes the lover beautiful? But God is always beautiful, never ugly, never changeable. He who is always beautiful has loved us first. And what sort of persons has he loved if not those who are loathsome and ugly? He didn't do so in order to leave them loathsome but in order to change them and, from being ugly, to make them beautiful. How shall we be beautiful? By loving him who is always beautiful. Beauty grows in you to the extent that love grows, because charity itself is the soul's beauty.

Let us love, because he loved us first. Listen to the apostle Paul: *But God showed his love for us because, when we were still sinners, Christ died for us* (Rom 5:8-9), the righteous for the unrighteous, the beautiful for the loathsome. How do we find that Jesus is beautiful? *Splendid in*

---

13. I.e., the beautiful woman.

form beyond the sons of men, grace is poured forth on your lips (Ps 45:2). How? See again how it is that he is beautiful: *Splendid in form beyond the sons of men,* because *in the beginning was the Word, and the Word was with God, and the Word was God* (Jn 1:1).[14]

But, because he took on flesh, he took on as it were your loathsomeness—that is, your mortality—in order to accommodate himself to you and to be suited to you and to arouse you to love beauty inwardly. How, then, do we find that Jesus is loathsome and ugly, as we have found that he is beautiful and *splendid in form beyond the sons of men?* How do we find that he is also ugly? Ask Isaiah. *And we saw him, and he had neither splendor nor comeliness* (Is 53:2).

These are the two pipes that, as it were, make different sounds, but one Spirit fills them both. By the one it is said, *Splendid in form beyond the sons of men;* by the other it is said in Isaiah, *We saw him, and he had neither splendor nor comeliness.* By the one Spirit both pipes are filled, and they aren't discordant. Don't avert your ears; use your understanding. Let us question the apostle Paul, and let him explain to us the harmony of the two pipes. Let him sound forth for us: *Splendid in form beyond the sons of men: Who, although he was in the form of God, did not consider it robbery to be equal to God* (Phil 2:6). There is the *splendid in form beyond the sons of men.* Let him also sound forth for us: *We saw him, and he had neither splendor nor comeliness. He emptied himself, taking the form of a slave, having been made in the likeness of men, and having been found in appearance as a man* (Phil 2:7). *He had neither splendor nor comeliness* so that he might give you splendor and comeliness. Which splendor? Which comeliness? The love of charity, so that as you love you may run, and as you run you may love. You are already beautiful. But don't look to yourself, lest you forfeit what you have received. Look to him by whom you have been made beautiful. May you be beautiful so that he may love you. But focus your attention entirely on him, run to him, beseech his embraces, fear to part from him, so that there may be in you the chaste fear that abides forever. *Let us love, because he loved us first.*

---

14. Christ's beauty is his divinity. Augustine also discusses this in *Holy Virginity* 55.

10. *If anyone says, I love God* (4:20). Which God? Why do we love? Because he loved us first and bestowed on us the means of loving. He loved the wicked so as to make them good; he loved the unrighteous so as to make them righteous; he loved the sick so as to make them healthy. Let us, then, also love, *because he loved us first.* Question someone; let him tell you if he loves God. He cries out, he confesses, "I love him; he knows it." There is something else to be asked. *If anyone says,* he says, *I love God, and hates his brother, he is a liar* (4:20). How do you tell that he is a liar? Listen: *For how can he who does not love his brother, whom he sees, love God, whom he does not see?* (4:20) What then? Does he who loves his brother also love God? It must be that he loves God; it must be that he loves love itself. Can he love his brother and not love love? It must be that he loves love. What then? Does he love God because he loves love? Precisely. By loving love he loves God. Or have you forgotten that you said a little earlier, *God is love?* If God is love, whoever loves love loves God. Love your brother, then, and be secure. You can't say, "I love my brother, but I don't love God." Just as you are lying if you say, "I love God," when you don't love your brother, so you are mistaken when you say, "I love my brother," if you are aware that you don't love God. It must be that you who love your brother love love itself. *Love is God.* It must be, then, that whoever loves God loves his brother. But if you don't love the brother whom you see, how can you love God, whom you don't see? Why doesn't a person see God? Because he doesn't have that love. He doesn't see God because he doesn't have love. He doesn't have love because he doesn't love his brother. Therefore, because he doesn't have love, he doesn't see God. For, if he has love, he sees God, because *God is love,* and his eye is ever more cleansed by love, so that he may see that unchangeable substance in whose presence he may always rejoice, which, once he has been united to the angels, he may enjoy forever. But let him hasten now so that sometime he may be gladdened in his homeland. Let him not love the pilgrimage, let him not love the way. Let everything be bitter apart from him who calls us, until we are joined to him, and let us say what is said in the psalm: *You have destroyed all those who fornicate away from you* (Ps 73:27). And who are those who fornicate? Those who depart and love the world. But what about you? In what follows it says, *But my good is to be joined to God* (Ps 73:28). My entire good is to

be freely joined to God. For, suppose that you ask and say, "Why are you joined to God?" and he says, "So that he may give me something."[15] What will he give you? He made heaven, he made the earth. What is he going to give you? Already you are joined to him. Find something better, and he gives it to you.

11. *For how can he who does not love his brother, whom he sees, love God, whom he does not see? And we have this command from him, that he who loves God must also love his brother.* (4:20-21) You said grandly, "I love God," and you hate your brother. O murderer, how do you love God? Didn't you hear previously in this very epistle, *He who hates his brother is a murderer* (3:15)? "But I do in fact love God, although I hate my brother." In fact you don't love God if you hate your brother. And I prove it now from another passage. He said, *He gave us a commandment to love one another* (3:23). How do you love him whose commandment you hate? Who is it that would say, "I love the emperor but I hate his laws"? This is how the emperor knows if you love him, if his laws are observed throughout the provinces. What is the emperor's law? *A new commandment I give you, that you love one another* (Jn 13:34). You say, then, that you love Christ. Keep his commandment and love your brother. But, if you don't love your brother, how do you love him whose commandment you disdain?

Brothers, I am never tired of speaking about charity in the name of Christ. To the degree that you are avaricious for this thing, we hope that it increases in you and casts out fear, so that the chaste fear which abides forever may remain. Let us endure the world, let us endure tribulations, let us endure the scandals of trials. Let us not turn aside from the way. Let us hold onto the unity of the Church, let us hold onto Christ, let us hold onto charity. Let us not be torn away from the members of his bride, let us not be torn away from the faith, so that we may glory in his presence, and we shall remain secure in him, now through faith and then through sight, the pledge of which we have as the gift of the Holy Spirit.

---

15. It is presumably the psalmist who is being asked and who responds here.

Tenth Homily

1. I believe that you who were here yesterday remember how far our homily went as we progressed in this epistle—namely, *For how can he who does not love his brother, whom he sees, love God, whom he does not see? And we have this commandment from him, that he who loves God must also love his brother.* (4:20-21) Our discussion went as far as that point. Let us see, then, what follows in sequence.

Everyone who believes that Jesus is the Christ has been born of God (5:1). Who is it that doesn't believe that Jesus is the Christ? He who doesn't live as Christ commanded. For there are many who say, "I believe," but faith without works doesn't save. But faith's work is love itself, as the apostle Paul says: *And the faith that works through love* (Gal 5:6). And, indeed, your past works, before you believed, either were nothing or, if they seemed good, were valueless. For, if they were nothing, you were like a man without feet or, with injured feet, unable to walk. But, if they seemed good, you were indeed able to run before you believed, but, because you weren't running on the way, you were going astray rather than arriving at your destination. For, as far as we are concerned, then, there is both running and running on the way. He who is not running on the way is running in vain; indeed, he is running to toil. The less he runs on the way, the more he goes astray. What is the way on which we are running? Christ said, *I am the way* (Jn 14:6). What is the homeland to which we are running? Christ said, *I am the truth* (Jn 14:6). You run *on* him, you run *to* him in whom you take your rest. But, so that we may run on him, he stretches himself to us, for we were far away, and we were journeying far away. It is not enough that we were journeying far away; we were also weak and unable to move ourselves. The physician came to the sick; the way was extended to the travelers. Let us be saved by him; let us walk by means of him.

This is what it means to believe that Jesus is the Christ, as Christians believe, who are Christians not only in name but also in deeds and life. That isn't how the demons believe. For even *the demons believe, and they tremble* (Jas 2:19), as scripture says. What more were the demons able to believe than what they said: *We know who you are: the Son of God* (Mk 1:24; Mt 8:29)? Peter also said what the demons said. When the Lord asked him who he was and what people called him, the disciples responded to him, *Some call you John the Baptist, others Elijah, still others Jeremiah or one of the prophets.* And he said, *But who do you say that I am?* Peter responded and said, *You are the Christ, the Son of the living God.* And from the Lord he heard, *Blessed are you, Simon Bar-Jonah, because flesh and blood has not revealed this to you, but my Father who is in heaven.* See what praises follow upon this faith: *You are Peter, and upon this rock I shall build my Church.* (Mt 16:14-18) What does this mean: *Upon this rock I shall build my Church?* Upon this faith, upon what was said: *You are the Christ, the Son of the living God. Upon this rock,* he says, *I shall establish my Church.* Great praise! And so Peter says, *You are the Christ, the Son of the living God,* and the demons also say, *We know who you are: the Son of God, the holy one of God.* This is what Peter says, and this is also what the demons say. The words are the same, but the intention isn't the same. And how is it evident that Peter said this with love? Because a Christian's faith is with love, whereas a demon's is without love. How is it without love? Peter said this in order to embrace Christ; the demons said this in order that Christ would depart from them. For, before they said, *We know who you are: you are the Son of God. What is that to us and to you?* they said, *Why have you come before the time to destroy us?* (Mt 8:29)[1] It is one thing, then, to confess Christ so that you may hold onto Christ; it is something else to confess Christ so that you may push Christ away from yourself.

You see, then, that, from the way [John] says here, *who believes,*[2] faith has a certain personal quality and is not, as it were, something crowd-like. And so, brothers, let none of the heretics say to you, "And we believe." For that is why I gave the example of the demons, so that you may not rejoice at the words of believers but test the deeds of the living.

---

1. Contrary to what Augustine says, he has in fact reversed the sequence of these two phrases.
2. As in *everyone who believes that Jesus is the Christ....*

2. Let us see, then, what it means to believe in Christ, what it means to believe that Jesus himself is the Christ. There follows: *Everyone who believes that Jesus is the Christ has been born of God.* But what does it mean to believe this? *And everyone who loves the one who has begotten him loves him who has been begotten by him* (5:1). He has joined love directly to faith, because faith is empty without love. With love it is the faith of a Christian; without love it is the faith of a demon. But those who don't believe are worse than demons and duller than demons. Some person or other doesn't want to believe in Christ; at that point he doesn't even imitate the demons. He already believes in Christ, but he hates Christ. He possesses a confession of faith in the fear of punishment, not in the love of the crown. For they also feared to be punished. Add love to this faith, so that it may become a faith of the sort that the apostle Paul calls *the faith that works through love*: you have found a Christian, you have found a citizen of Jerusalem, you have found a [fellow] citizen of the angels, you have found a traveler who is yearning on his journey. Join yourself to him; he is your companion; run with him if you are still this as well. *Everyone who loves the one who has begotten him loves him who has been begotten by him.* Who has begotten? The Father. Who has been begotten? The Son. What, then, is he saying? Everyone who loves the Father loves the Son.

3. *This is how we know that we love the sons of God* (5:2). What is this, brothers? A short while before he was speaking of the Son of God, not of the sons of God. See, one Christ has been proposed for us to contemplate, and it has been said to us, *Everyone who believes that Jesus is the Son of God has been born of God, and everyone who loves the one who has begotten him*—that is, the Father—*loves him who has been begotten by him*—that is, the Son, our Lord Jesus Christ. And there follows: *This is how we know that we love the sons of God.* It is as though he were going to say, "This is how we know that we love the Son of God." He who shortly before was saying *the Son of God* said *the sons of God*, because the sons of God are the body of the only Son of God, and, since he is the head and we are the members, the Son of God is one. Therefore, he who loves the sons of God loves the Son of God, and he who loves the Son of God loves

the Father. Nor can anyone love the Father unless he loves the Son, and he who loves the Son also loves the sons of God.

Which sons of God? The members of the Son of God. And he himself also becomes a member by loving, and through love he comes to be in the structure of Christ's body, and there shall be one Christ loving himself. For, when the members love each other, the body loves itself.[3] *And, if one member suffers, all the members suffer with it; and, if one member is glorified, all the members rejoice with it* (1 Cor 12:26). And what does he say next? *But you are the body of Christ and his members* (1 Cor 12:27). He was speaking shortly before of brotherly love, and he said, *How will he who does not love his brother, whom he sees, be able to love God, whom he does not see?* (4:20) But, if you love your brother, perhaps you love your brother and don't love Christ? How can that be, when you love Christ's members? When you love Christ's members, then, you love Christ; when you love Christ, you love the Son of God; when you love the Son of God, you also love his Father. Love, then, cannot be separated. Choose for yourself what to love; other things come to you as a result. Should you say, "I love God alone, God the Father," you are lying. If you love, you don't love one thing alone, but, if you love the Father, you also love the Son. "See," you say, "I love the Father and I love the Son, but them alone: God the Father and God the Son and our Lord Jesus Christ, who ascended into heaven and is seated at the right hand of the Father —that Word through whom all things were made, and the Word was made flesh and dwelled among us.[4] Them alone I love." You are lying, for, if you love the head, you also love the members; but, if you don't love the members, neither do you love the head. Aren't you terrified at the voice of the head crying out from heaven on behalf of his members, *Saul, Saul, why are you persecuting me?* (Acts 9:4) He called the persecutor of his members his own persecutor; he called the lover of his members his own lover. You already know what his members are, brothers; it is God's Church itself.

---

3. Burnaby and Rettig single out this sentence for its succinct statement of the unity of Christ and his Church.
4. See Jn 1:3-14.

This is how we know that we love the sons of God, because we love God (5:2). And how? Aren't the sons of God one thing and God something else? But he who loves God loves his commandments. And what are God's commandments? *A new commandment I give you, that you love one another* (Jn 13:34). Let no one dispense himself from one love for the sake of another love. This is how this love is held fast in its entirety: just as it is joined in a single unit, so all those who depend on it make up a single unit, and it is as though fire fuses them. It is gold: a lump is fused, and it becomes a single something. But, unless the heat of charity blazes up, there can be no fusion of many into one. Because we love God, that is how we know that we love the sons of God.

4. And how do we know that we love the sons of God? *Because we love God, and we carry out his commandments* (5:2). Here we sigh over the difficulties of carrying out God's commandment. Listen to what follows. Man, what are you exerting yourself for by loving? By loving avarice? What you love is loved with exertion. God is loved without exertion. Avarice will summon up exertion, dangers, exhaustion, troubles, and you are going to submit to this! To what end? You forsake your peace so as to have something to fill up your treasure chest. Perhaps you had greater peace before you possessed than when you began to possess. See what avarice has imposed upon you: you have filled your house and thieves make you afraid; you have acquired gold and lost your sleep. See what avarice has imposed on you: "Do it," and you did it. What does God command you to do? "Love me. You love gold; you are about to look for gold and perhaps you won't find it. Whoever looks for me, I am with him. You are about to love honor and perhaps you won't attain to it. Who has loved me and not attained to me?" God tells you, "You want to locate a patron or a powerful friend for yourself; you seek entrée by way of someone else who is inferior. Love me," God tells you. "There is no entrée with me through someone else. Love itself makes me present to you." What is sweeter than this love, brothers? Not without reason, brothers, did you recently hear in the psalm: *The unrighteous told me of their pleasures, but not like your law, Lord* (Ps 119:85). What is God's law? God's commandment. What is God's commandment? That new

commandment which is called new because it introduces something new: *A new commandment I give you, that you love one another.* Listen to what God's law itself is: the Apostle says, *Bear one another's burdens, and thus you will fulfill the law of Christ* (Gal 6:2). Love itself is the fulfillment of all our works. That is where the end is; on its account we run; when we arrive at it we rest.

5. You have heard in the psalm: *I have seen the end of all fulfillment* (Ps 119:96). [The psalmist] said, *I have seen the end of all fulfillment.* What did he see? Do we think that he ascended to the summit of some very high and steep mountain and looked around and saw the edge of the earth and the heavenly bodies in orbit, and that therefore he said, *I have seen the end of all fulfillment*? If this is praiseworthy, let us ask the Lord for eyes of flesh that are so sharp that we would need some very high mountain, which is on earth, from whose peak we might see the end of all fulfillment. Don't go far. See, I tell you, go up the mountain and see the end. Christ is the mountain. Come to Christ; from there you see the end of all fulfillment. What is that end? Ask Paul. *But the end of the commandment is charity from a pure heart, and a good conscience, and an unfeigned faith* (1 Tim 1:5); and, in another passage: *But the fullness of the law is charity* (Rom 13:10). What is so ended and completed as fullness? Hence, brothers, [the psalmist] uses *end* in a praiseworthy manner. Do not think of consumption but of finishing.[5] For otherwise it is said, "I have made an end of the bread," and still otherwise, "I have ended the tunic."[6] I have made an end of the bread by eating it; I have ended the tunic by weaving it. "End" is found in the one and "end" is found in the other, but nonetheless the bread is made an end of by being consumed and the tunic is ended by being finished; the bread is made an end of so that it doesn't exist, and the tunic is ended by being completed. That is how you should hear *end*, when the psalm is being read and you hear, *Unto the end, a psalm of David.* You hear this constantly in the psalms, and you ought to know what you are hearing. What does *unto the end*

---

5. "Consumption ... finishing": *consumptionem ... consummationem.*

6. "Made an end ... have ended": *finivi ... finivi.* It would be more colloquial in each case to translate "I have finished," but this translation includes the noun "end" (*finis*) or its verbal equivalent, both of which Augustine has been using.

mean?[7] *For the end of the law is Christ, unto righteousness for everyone who believes* (Rom 13:10). And what does "Christ the end" mean? That Christ is God, and the end of the commandment is charity, and God is charity; that the Father and the Son and the Holy Spirit are one. That is where the end is for you; elsewhere he is the way. Don't cling to the way and not arrive at the end. Whatever else you may have come to, pass beyond it until you arrive at the end. What is the end? *But my good is to cling to God* (Ps 73:28). You have clung to God, you have come to the end of the way, you shall abide in the homeland.

Pay heed. Someone is seeking money; let that not be your end: pass on like a wayfarer. Seek where you may pass on to, not where you may remain. But if you love it, you are entangled by avarice. Avarice will be your leg chains; you are unable to go further. Pass on, then, beyond this as well. Seek the end. You seek health of body, yet don't remain there. For what is this health of body, which is extinguished by death, which is weakened by illness, which is frivolous, mortal, fluid? Seek it, lest perhaps ill health impede your good works. The end isn't there, then, because it is being sought for the sake of something else. Whatever is being sought for the sake of something else, the end isn't there. Whatever is being sought for its own sake and freely, the end is there. Are you seeking honors? Perhaps you are seeking for something to be done, so that you may accomplish something, so that you may please God. Don't love the honor itself, lest you remain there. Are you seeking praise? If you are seeking God's, you are doing well; if you are seeking your own, you are doing badly. Remain on the way. But see, *you* are being loved, *you* are being praised. Don't be grateful when you are being praised in yourself. Praise in the Lord, so that you may sing, *My soul shall be praised in the Lord* (Ps 34:2). Do you utter some good discourse, and is

---

7. *Unto the end: in finem. In finem* was the common way of translating into Latin the Hebrew letter *lamed*, which is part of the superscription of many psalms. At least six different prepositional meanings are given for it; see Peter C. Craigie, *Psalms 1-50* = Word Biblical Commentary 19 (Waco, Texas: Word Books, 1983) 34. Augustine's understanding of the letter's Latin translation is entirely allegorical and has nothing to do with the Hebrew original; see also *Exposition of Psalm* 4,1.

your discourse praised?[8] Don't let it be praised as yours; the end isn't there. If that is where you place the end, you are ended, but you aren't ended as though you are being perfected, but you are ended as though you are being consumed. Hence, don't let your discourse be praised as though it were from you, as though it were yours. But how should it be praised? As the psalm says: *In God I shall praise my discourse, in God I shall praise my word* (Ps 56:4). The result of this is that what follows may happen in you: *In God I have hoped; I do not fear what man may do to me* (Ps 56:4 and 11). For when everything that is yours is praised in God, there is no fear that your praise will be destroyed, because God does not cease. Pass on, then, beyond this as well.

6. See, brothers, how many things we have passed beyond in which the end doesn't exist. We use these things as it were on the way; we are refreshed as it were by stopping in hostelries, and we pass on. Where, then, is the end? *Beloved, we are God's children, and what we shall be has not yet appeared* (3:2): this is said here, in this epistle. We are still on the way, therefore; as far as we may have come, we must pass on until we arrive at a particular end. *We know that, when he appears, we shall be like him, because we shall see him as he is* (3:2). That is the end; there is the perpetual praise, there always the unceasing Alleluia.

[The psalmist] spoke, then, of this very end in the psalm: *I have seen the end of all fulfillment.* And, as though it were being said to him, "What is the end that you have seen?" [he continues,] *Your commandment is broad indeed* (Ps 119:96). This itself is the end, the breadth of the commandment. The breadth of the commandment is charity, because, where there is charity, there is no narrowness.[9] The Apostle was in that very breadth when he said, *Our mouth is open to you, O Corinthians; our heart has been enlarged; you are not made narrow in us* (2 Cor 6:11-12).

---

8. "Discourse": *sermo. Sermo* can be used for numerous things in addition to discourse (which suggests a public utterance), such as ordinary conversation, disputation, and even simply a word. Of course it can also mean "sermon," as in I,5, and Augustine almost certainly intended the ambiguity to allow for including himself in his admonition, since his sermons were subject to praise.

9. "Narrowness": *angustiae*, which also means "troubles" or "difficulties," which likewise suits the context.

And so, therefore, *your commandment is broad indeed.* What is the broad commandment? *A new commandment I give you, that you love one another.* Charity, therefore, is not made narrow. Do you want not to be made narrow on earth? Dwell in breadth. For, whatever a person may have done to you, it doesn't make you narrow, because you love what a human being doesn't harm: you love God, you love the brotherhood, you love God's law, you love God's Church; it shall be forever. You are toiling on earth, but you shall come to the promised fruition. Who takes away from you what you love? If no one takes away from you what you love, you sleep securely; or rather you stay awake securely, lest by sleeping you lose what you love. For it isn't said in vain: *Enlighten my eyes, lest at any time I fall asleep in death* (Ps 13:3). Those who close their eyes against charity fall asleep in the concupiscences of fleshly pleasures. Stay awake, then. For these are pleasures—eating, drinking, living extravagantly, playing games, hunting; every evil follows these vain displays. Don't we know that these are pleasures? Who would deny that they give pleasure? But God's law is more loveable. Cry out against persuaders of this sort: *The unrighteous told me of their pleasures, but not like your law, Lord.* This is the pleasure that remains. It not only remains wherever you may come but even calls back the one who is fleeing.

7. *For the love of God is this, that we observe his commandments* (5:3). You have already heard: *On these two commandments the whole law depends, and also the prophets* (Mt 22:40). How [God] didn't want you to be scattered among many pages! *On these two commandments the whole law depends, and also the prophets.* On which two commandments? *You shall love the Lord your God from your whole heart, and from your whole soul, and from your whole mind,* and *you shall love your neighbor as yourself. On these two commandments the whole law depends, and also the prophets.* (Mt 22:33.39-40) See, the whole of this epistle speaks of these commandments. Hold onto love, then, and be secure. Why do you fear that you might do something bad to someone? Who does anything bad to someone that he loves? If you love, nothing can happen apart from doing good.

But perhaps you make a correction. It is love that does this, not anger. But perhaps you administer a beating. You do this for the sake of discipline, because love of love itself doesn't allow you to neglect someone who is undisciplined. And in a certain way something like a different and contrary result is effected, so that sometimes hatred is flattering and charity is angry. Someone or other hates his enemy and makes believe that he is his friend: he sees him doing something bad and he praises him. He wants him to be heedless; he wants him to go blindly among the precipices of his cupidities, from which he may perhaps not return. He praises him, *because the sinner is praised in the desires of his soul* (Ps 10:3). He applies to him the unction of his own adulation. See, he hates him and he praises him. Someone else sees his friend doing something of the same sort, and he recalls him. If he doesn't hear him, he even chastises him orally, he rebukes him, he withstands him. At a given moment there arrives the need to withstand him. See, hatred is flattering and charity withstands. Don't look to a flatterer's words or to what seems to be a rebuker's anger. Consider the source; seek the root whence it proceeds. The one flatters so as to deceive, the other withstands so as to correct.

There is no need, therefore, brothers, for your heart to be enlarged by us. Ask God that you may love one another. You should love all people, even your enemies, not because they are your brothers but so that they may become your brothers, so that you may always be aflame with brotherly love, whether towards one who has become your brother or towards your enemy, so that by loving him he may become your brother. Wherever you love a brother, you love a friend. He is already with you; he has already been joined to you as well in Catholic unity. If you live rightly, you love the one who has become your brother from having been your enemy. If[10] you love someone who doesn't yet believe in Christ, or, if he has believed in Christ, believes as the demons do, you are reproaching his vanity. As far as you yourself are concerned, love, and love with brotherly love. He isn't yet a brother, but you love him so that he may be a brother. All our brotherly love, then, is directed towards Christians, towards all his members. My brothers, the discipline, the strength, the

---

10. Reading *si* ("if") rather than *sed* ("but"). Perhaps, however, the *si* was dropped at some point, in which case the original would have been *sed si* ("but if").

blooms, the fruits, the beauty, the delight, the sustenance, the food, the drink, the embrace of charity is beyond satiety. If it so pleases us wayfarers, how shall we be gladdened in the homeland!

8. Let us run, then, my brothers, let us run and let us love Christ. Which Christ? Jesus Christ. Who is he? The Word of God. And how did he come to those who were sick? *The Word was made flesh and dwelled among us* (Jn 1:14). What scripture predicted, then, has been fulfilled: *Christ had to suffer and on the third day rise from the dead* (Lk 24:46). Where does his body lie? Where do his members toil? Where should you be, so that you may be under his head? *And in his name penance and the remission of sins would be preached throughout all the nations, beginning from Jerusalem* (Lk 24:47). That is where your charity should be poured out. Christ and the psalm—that is, the Holy Spirit—says, *Your commandment is broad indeed.* And somebody or other is placing the boundaries of charity in Africa![11] Spread your charity throughout the world, if you want to love Christ, because Christ's members lie throughout the world. If you love a section, you have been cut off; if you have been cut off, you aren't in the body; if you aren't in the body, you aren't under the head.

What good does it do you to believe and to blaspheme? You love him in his head, you blaspheme him in his body. He loves his body. If you have cut yourself off from his body, the head hasn't cut himself off from his body. "You honor me to no avail," cries out the head from on high. It is as though someone wanted to kiss your head and to trample on your feet. Perhaps he would crush your feet with nailed boots, while wanting to hold your head and kiss it. Wouldn't you cry out and say, "What are you doing, man? You're trampling on me," as the person honoring you was speaking? You wouldn't say, "You're trampling on my head," because he was honoring your head. But your head would cry out more on behalf of its members than for its own sake, because it was being honored. Doesn't the head itself cry out, "I don't want your honor; don't trample on me"? Now say if you can, "Why have I trampled on you?" Tell this to the head: "I wanted to kiss you, I wanted to embrace you." But don't you see, O fool, that, because of a kind of structural unity, what you want to embrace

---

11. Augustine is referring to the Donatists, who were almost entirely confined to Africa.

reaches all the way to what you are trampling on? You honor me up above, you trample on me down below. There is more pain in what you are trampling on than there is joy in what you are honoring, because what you are honoring is pained on account of those whom you are trampling on. How does your tongue cry out? "It hurts me." It doesn't say, "It hurts my foot," but it says, "It hurts *me*." O tongue, who touched you? Who struck you? Who disturbed you? Who troubled you? "No one, but I am joined to those that are being trampled on. How is it that you don't want me to be pained when I'm not separate?"

9. Our Lord Jesus Christ, then, when he ascended into heaven on the fortieth day, commended his body, where he would have a place to lie, for the reason that he saw the many who were going to honor him because he ascended into heaven, and he saw that the honor of those persons is useless if they tread down his members on earth. And, so that no one would err and, while adoring the head in heaven, trample on the feet on earth, he said where his members would be. For, as he was about to ascend, he spoke his last words; after those words he didn't speak on earth. The head, as he was about to ascend into heaven, commended his members on earth, and he departed. No more do you find Christ speaking on earth; you find him speaking—but from heaven. And why from heaven itself? Because on earth his members were being trampled on. For from on high he said to the persecutor Saul, *Saul, Saul, why are you persecuting me?* (Acts 9:4) "I have ascended into heaven, but I am still lying on earth. Here I sit at the Father's right hand; there I am still hungry, thirsty and a traveler." How, then, as he was about to ascend, did he commend his body on earth? When his disciples asked him, *Lord, will you be made present at this time, and when will be the kingdom of Israel?* (Acts 1:6), he replied as he was about to go, *It is not for you to know the time that the Father chose in his authority, but you shall receive the power of the Holy Spirit coming upon you, and you shall be my witnesses* (Acts 1:7-8). See where he spreads his body, see where he doesn't want to be trampled on: *You shall be my witnesses in Jerusalem, and in all of Judea and Samaria and to the ends of the earth* (Acts 1:8). "See where I who am ascending lie. For I am ascending because I am the head. My

body still lies. Where does it lie? Throughout the earth. Beware lest you strike, beware lest you violate, beware lest you trample down." These are Christ's last words as he was about to go to heaven.

Imagine a man who is weak and in bed, lying at home and wasting away with sickness, close to death, breathing with difficulty, having his soul to a certain degree already between his teeth, who is perhaps worried about something that is precious to him, which he loves a great deal. It comes into his mind, and he summons his heirs and says, "I ask you: do this." He clings fiercely to his soul, so to say, lest he depart before these words are uttered. Once he has spoken these last words, he breathes out his soul. The corpse is carried to its grave. How do his heirs remember the dying man's last words? How, if someone appeared who would say to them, "Don't do it"? What would they say then? Do I not then do what my father commanded me as he finally breathed out his soul, what was the last thing that sounded in my ears as my father departed from here? Whatever other words of his I may otherwise have, his final words hold me most in their grip. I did not see him or hear him speak any more.

Brothers, consider with Christian hearts if there are words as dear, as moving, as weighty as those of one who is about to go to his grave. For the heirs of Christ, who was not about to go back to his grave but about to ascend into heaven, that is how his last words should be. For he who has lived and died, his soul is taken off to other places and his body is put in the ground. Whether those words come to pass or don't come to pass has nothing to do with him. Now he is doing one thing or enduring another: either he is rejoicing in the bosom of Abraham or he is yearning for a drop of water in eternal fire.[12] In either case his corpse is lying without feeling in the grave, and the last words of the dying man are being kept. What do they hope for themselves who don't keep the last words of him who is seated in heaven, of him who sees from on high whether they are disdained or not disdained, of him who said, *Saul, Saul, why are you persecuting me?* and who reserves for judgment whatever he sees that his members are suffering?

---

12. See Lk 16:22.

10. "And what have we done?" they say. "We have endured persecution; we haven't caused it."[13] You *have* caused it, O wretches—first, because you have divided the Church. The sword of the tongue is greater than that of iron.

Sarah's maidservant Hagar was proud, and she was mistreated by her mistress because of her pride. That was discipline, not punishment. Hence, when she had left her mistress, what did the angel tell her? *Return to your mistress* (Gn 16:9). If perhaps you, then, fleshly soul, have, like the proud maidservant, endured a few vexations, why are you disturbed? Go back to your mistress, grasp the Lord's peace. See, the gospels are brought forth; we read where the Church is spread out. An argument is raised against us and we are called betrayers.[14] Betrayers with regard to what? Christ commends his Church, and you don't believe. Shall I believe you when you slander my forebears? Do you want me to believe you concerning betrayers? Believe in Christ first. What is worthy? Christ is God, you are a human being. Who ought to be believed first? Christ has spread his Church throughout the earth. For myself, I say, "Disregard me." The gospel speaks. Beware! What does the gospel say? *Christ had to suffer and rise from the dead on the third day, and in his name penance and the remission of sins would be preached.* Where there is the remission of sins, there is the Church. How is the Church there? It was said to her, *To you I shall give the keys of the kingdom of heaven, and what you loose on earth shall be loosed also in heaven, and what you bind on earth shall be bound also in heaven* (Mt 16:19). Where is this remission of sins spread? *Throughout all the nations, beginning from Jerusalem.* See: believe Christ. But because you understand, if you believe in Christ, that there is nothing for you to say regarding betrayers, you want me to believe you when you slander my forebears rather than that you should believe Christ when he preaches....[15]

---

13. Augustine intends us to understand that the Donatists are saying this. He addresses them in what follows.

14. "Betrayers": *traditores*. The term goes back to the origins of Donatism in the early fourth century, when some members of the Carthaginian clergy were accused of having handed over (*tradere*) sacred books during the persecution of Diocletian. See the imperial documentation cited in Augustine, Letter 88,4.

15. The sermon ends abruptly here, and it is obviously incomplete.

Index of Scripture

(prepared by Michael T. Dolan)

1:7-8	X, 9	Galatians	
1:8	X, 9	1:22-24	VIII, 2
2:4	II, 3	2:20	VII, 7
9:4	X, 3; X, 9	5:6	X, 1
		6:2	I, 12; X, 4
Romans		6:4	VI, 2
1:17	IV, 8		
1:24	VI, 8	Ephesians	
1:25	II, 11	3:8	VIII, 2
2:21	VI, 14	3:17	II, 9
3:4	I, 6	4:2-3	I, 12
5:5	VI, 8; VII, 6; VIII, 12	5:8	I, 10
5:8-9	IX, 9		
8:24	VIII, 13	Philippians	
8:24-25	IV, 7	1:21-24	V, 4
8:26-27	VI, 8	1:23	IX, 2
8:32	VII, 7	1:23-24	IX, 2
8:35	IX, 4	2:6	IV, 5; IX, 9
13:8	V, 7	2:7	IX, 9
13:10	V, 7; X, 5	3:12-13	IV, 6
		3:13-14	IV, 6
1 Corinthians		Colossians	
1:13	II, 4	3:5	IX, 2
2:9	IV, 5; VII, 1	3:9-10	I, 10
3:6-7	III, 13	4:3	I, 8
4:3	VI, 2		
4:15	V, 7	1 Thessalonians	
7:7	VIII, 8	2:7	IX, 1
8:1	II, 8		
11:29	VII, 6	1 Timothy	
12:26	III, 4; X, 3	1:5	X, 5
12:27	X, 3	6:10	VIII, 6
13:2	V, 6		
13:3	VI, 2; VIII, 9	Titus	
13:4	V, 8	1:16	III, 8; VI, 13
13:8	IX, 1		
15:9	VIII, 2	Hebrews	
		12:6	VIII, 7
2 Corinthians		13:1	VIII, 3
1:12	VI, 2		
6:11-12	VI, 5; X, 6	James	
6:14	I, 5	2:19	X, 1
11:29	I, 12		
12:7-9	VI, 6	1 Peter	
12:15	V, 4; VI, 2; VI, 5	3:13	IX, 4
		4:8	I, 6; V, 3

General Index

(prepared by Kathleen Strattan)

demons, I,11, 13; II,8, 13; VI,7; X,1–2, 7
  See also angels of the devil
  faith of, II,8; X,1–2
  prayer of, VI,7
denial of Christ. *See under* Jesus Christ:
  denial of
desire, holy, IV,6
desire of the flesh/eyes, II,10, 12–14; VII,10
devil, I,5; II,6–7, 11, 14; IV,1–3; V,8; VII,2
  See also angels of the devil; demons;
    eternal fire; evil; serpent; sin
  Cain as from, V,8
  children of, V,7–8
  as the enemy, II,14; IV,3
  imitation of, IV,10
  and Job, VI,7
  sacraments of, II,13
  sin and, IV,10–12; V,2; VI,7
dilectio/diligere, VIII,5
  See also love
disciples, I,3; II,1–3; III,2; IV,2; V,4–5;
    VII,7; VIII,10; X,9
  See also apostles; *individual names;*
    specific topics
discipline, VII,8, 11; VIII,9; X,7, 10
discourse: praise for, X,5
disease. *See* sickness
dissolving, VI,14
division in the Church. *See* schism
doctors. *See* physicians
Donatist schism, I,8, 12; II,3–4, 8; VI,10;
    VII,11; X,10
  See also schism
  and betrayers *(traditores),* X,10
  as breach of charity, VII,11
  as geographically limited, I,8, 12–13;
    II,2–3; III,7; X,8, 10
  ideals of, I,8
  and martyrdom, VI,2
  rebaptism, VII,11
  and the sacraments, II,3; III,5; VII,11
Donatus, II,3–4
  See also Donatist schism, above
dove, VII,11
drunkenness, II,11; III,9; IV,4

ears, I,13; IV,9; VI,12; VIII,2
earth. *See* creation; world
Easter week, *Prologue;* I,13; II,1–2; IV,4;
    IX,2

the Eleven, II,1
  See also apostles
Elijah, V,5; X,1
"end," the term, X,5–6
enemies
  See also hatred
  as false friends, X,7
  love for, I,9–11; VIII,4, 10–11; IX,3,
    9; X,7
  prayer for, I,9; IX,3
  sins as, IX,2
  souls of, healing, VIII,11
  wishing good for, I,9; VIII,10
enemy, Satan as, II,14; IV,3
enjoyment. *See* joy; pleasure
enlightenment, I,4, 6; IV,8; X,6
envy, V,8, 10; VIII,8
equality
  See also under Son: as equal to the
    Father
  among people, VIII,5, 8
error, II,1; VII,4, 11
  See also heresy; schism; sin
eternal fire, III,11–12; IV,2, 5; IX,5; X,9
  See also hell
eternal life, I,3, 5, 12; III,11–12; V,3;
    VIII,14
  See also heaven; immortality
  and answering of prayer, VI,6
  enemies and, V,10; VIII,10–11
  wishing for others, VIII,5, 10
eternity, II,5, 10
  See also under God: as eternal
eucharist, I,2, 9, 12; II,1; III,5; VII,6;
    VIII,10
  See also sacraments
  the wicked and, VII,6
Eunomians, VI,12
Eve, IV,3
evil, I,7, 12; VI,7; IX,2, 5; X,6
  See also devil; sin; *specific topics,*
    e.g., lies
  charity and, II,8
  deeds, II,13
  desires, VIII,6
  *The face of the Lord is over those who
    do evil,* IX,7
  greatness of, VIII,14
  left hand, VI,3
  love of the world as, II,9

of God for us, VII,7, 9; VIII,10;
IX,9–10
as God ("love is God"), VII,6; IX,10
the greatest, V,11–12; VI,1–2, 13;
VII,2, 7
as harsh, VII,8, 11; X,7
Holy Spirit and, VI,8–11; VII,6;
VIII,1, 12; X,8
and judgment day, IX,2–4
and knowledge, II,8
lack of, V,10
and the law, V,7; X,4–7
and life vs. death, V,10
for love, IX,10
love, and do what you want, VII,8
maintaining, VII,11
for neighbor, V,7; VII,11; X,7
perfect, I,9; V,4–6, 11–12; VI,1–3, 13;
VII,2, 7; VIII,10, 12; IX,4
scripture and, V,13; VII,4–5
and sin, I,6; V,2–3
and tolerance, I,12
two loves, II,8–14 passim
and unity, I,12
wicked people and, VII,6
and works, VIII,9; X,4
for the world, II,8–14; V,9; VII,3;
IX,10
lust. *See* concupiscence; desire of the flesh

Maccabees, VIII,7
Macedonians, VI,12
magic, II,13
man. *See specific topics,* e.g., animals:
man's power over
man-man and man-God, IV,11
mark, V,6
marriage, I,2; II,2; III,7
See also bride and bridegroom
wives, adulterous vs. chaste, IX,6–7
martyrdom, I,2; V,4–5, 11; VIII,7, 9
the Donatists and, VI,2
Mary, the Virgin, I,1–2, 13; II,5
Mary Magdalene, III,2
men, II,6–7; III,2
mercy, I,9; II,10; V,12; VIII,1, 5, 9–11
See also works
works of, VIII,1, 5
milk, III,1; IX,1
miracles, II,13–14; VI,10; VIII,10

moderation, II,12
moon, I,4, 12–13; II,11; IV,5
morality: Donatists and, I,8
mortality, II,10; III,11; IV,3; V,5; VIII,7,
13; IX,9; X,5
See also flesh
Moses, II,1–2, 5–6
mother:
charity as, I,11; II,4; IX,1
Church as, III,1
mother of Jesus, II,5
mountain; mountains, I,8, 13; II,2; III,6; X,5
mule, horse and, VIII,6
murder. *See* killing
mystery. *See* sacrament (mystery)

neighbor, love for, V,7; VII,11; X,7
See also brotherly love
new life, I,5; II,5
the "new man," I,10
New Testament, V,3
See also gospel; scripture, sacred;
specific names, topics, and events
nonbelievers, X,7
North Africa. *See under* Donatist schism:
as limited to North Africa
Novatians, VI,12
numbers, II,3

offering, V,5, 8–9; VII,9
"old man" and "new man," I,10
Old Testament, II,1; VI,7
See also law; scripture, sacred;
specific names, topics, and events
as predicting Christ, II,1; X,8

paganism, I,11; II,13; V,12
particular sin. *See under* sin: particular
the Pasch, I,5
patience, IV,7; VIII,7; IX,2
Paul, II,4; VI,2, 5–10 passim; VIII,2
See also specific topics
transformation from Saul, VIII,2; X,3, 9
peace, *Prologue;* I,12–13; VI,10; VIII,5;
IX,8; X,4, 10
pearl, V,7
penance; penitence, II,2; III,7; X,8, 10
Pentecost, II,3; VI,10–11; VIII,10
perfection. *See under specific topics,* e.g.,
love; righteousness

sacred scripture. *See* scripture, sacred
sacrifice, V,8–9
"the pure victim," VII,9
saints, I,8; VI,6, 8
salvation, II,9; III,1, 9; IV,2, 7; V,2–5
     passim; VI,3–8 passim; VIII,13; X,1
     and fellowship with God, I,5
     and sacred scripture, II,1
     seeking our brother's, VI,4
sanctification, I,8
Sarah, X,10
Satan. *See* devil
Saul, King, VII,6; VIII,2
Saul (Paul), VIII,2; X,3, 9
     See also Paul
savior, Christ as, VIII,13
     See also Jesus Christ; Son
scandal, I,12; VII,5; IX,11
schism, I,12–13; II,1–4; III,4, 7, 9; VI,2,
     11–14
     See also Donatist schism; error; heresy
scripture, sacred, II,1–2; III,1; V,2
     See also New Testament; Old
          Testament; *specific topics*
     love in, V,13; VII,4–5
     and salvation, II,1
seducers, VII,11
seed, I,13; II,9; V,13
     of God, V,2, 7
serpent, III,2; VI,7
seventy men, I,12
sexual intercourse, I,13; II,12
sickness, V,5; VI,5, 8, 11, 13; VIII,2; X,5, 9
     See also health; physicians
     healing, II,14; VI,5; VII,7; VIII,11, 13;
          IX,10; X,8
signs, II,13; IV,2; VI,10
sin, I,5–8; V,3; VIII,6
     See also confession of sin; darkness;
          evil; forgiveness; wickedness;
          specific topics, e.g., envy; hatred;
          pride
     beginning of every, VIII,6
     in the Church, III,9
     definition of, V,3
     the devil and, IV,10–12; V,2; VI,7
     *Everyone who has been born from
          God does not sin,* V,2, 7
     freedom from, IV,11–12
     God's love for sinners, VIII,10

*If I had not come, they would not have
     sin,* VI,5
love and, I,6; V,2–3
     particular, V,2–3; VI,5
     pride and, VIII,6
     propitiation for, I,7–8; V,9
     and rebirth, V,1
     remission of, II,2; III,7; X,8, 10
     root of, V,2
     wickedness and, IV,8
slaves; slavery, VII,11; VIII,14
     blood of Christ and, I,5
     Christ in form of, IV,5; IX,9
     slave dealer, VII,7
sluggish people, IX,1
sobriety, IV,4; VIII,1
the Son, I,3–5; IV,9, 11; V,2; VII,2, 7, 9;
     VIII,14
     See also God; Jesus Christ; savior;
          specific topics, e.g., eucharist
     abiding in, III,11
     as alive forever, II,1
     co-heirs of, II,9; VIII,14; X,3
     commandments and, VI,9
     confession of, III,10; VIII,14; X,1
     demons confessing, II,8; X,1
     denial of, III,10
     as equal to the Father, II,1, 5; III,2;
          IV,5, 9; VI,12; IX,9
     eternal origin of, II,5
     Peter confessing, X,1
     sons, II,5–6
     of God, II,14; IV,4; IX,3; X,3–4
soul, V,3–4; VI,2, 5, 11; IX,2, 4, 6, 9; X,7
     of angels, IV,3
     beauty of, IX,9
     chaste, IX,2
     at death, X,9
     healing of enemy's, VIII,11
     and mortality, III,11
     stretching of, IV,6
     and temporal wellbeing, I,9
speech. *See* discourse; words
Spirit, Holy. *See* Holy Spirit
spirits:
     breath, IX,5
     Do not believe every spirit, VI,11–14
     prophetic, VII,6
     of truth and error, VII,4
stealing, VI,14; VII,10

THE COMPLETE WORKS OF ST. AUGUSTINE
A Translation for the 21st Century

Sermons 184-229 (III/6)
cloth, 978-1-56548-050-6

Sermons 230-272 (III/7)
cloth, 978-1-56548-059-9

Sermons 273-305A (III/8)
cloth, 978-1-56548-060-5

Sermons 306-340A (III/9)
cloth, 978-1-56548-068-1

Sermons 341-400 (III/10)
cloth, 978-1-56548-028-5

Sermons Newly Discovered Since 1990
(III/11)
cloth, 978-1-56548-103-9

Homilies on the Gospel of John 1-40
(III/12)
cloth, 978-1-56548-319-4
paper, 978-1-56548-318-7

Homilies on the Gospel of John (41-124)
(III/13) forthcoming

Homilies on the First Letter of John (III/14)
cloth, 978-1-56548-288-3
paper, 978-1-56548-289-0

Expositions of the Psalms 1-32 (III/15)
cloth, 978-1-56548-126-8
paper, 978-1-56548-140-4

Expositions of the Psalms 33-50 (III/16)
cloth, 978-1-56548-147-3
paper, 978-1-56548-146-6

Expositions of the Psalms 51-72 (III/17)
cloth, 978-1-56548-156-5
paper, 978-1-56548-155-8

Expositions of the Psalms 73-98 (III/18)
cloth, 978-1-56548-167-1
paper, 978-1-56548-166-4

Expositions of the Psalms 99-120 (III/19)
cloth, 978-1-56548-197-8
paper, 978-1-56548-196-1

Expositions of the Psalms 121-150 (III/20)
cloth, 978-1-56548-211-1
paper, 978-1-56548-210-4

Essential Texts Created for Classroom Use

Augustine Catechism: Enchiridion on Faith Hope and Love
paper, 978-1-56548-298-2

Essential Expositions of the Psalms
paper, 978-1-56548-510-5

Essential Sermons
paper, 978-1-56548-276-0

Instructing Beginners in Faith
paper, 978-1-56548-239-5

Monastic Rules
paper, 978-1-56548-130-5

Prayers from The Confessions
paper, 978-1-56548-188-6

Selected Writings on Grace and Pelagianism
paper, 978-1-56548-372-9

Soliloquies: Augustine's Inner Dialogue
paper, 978-1-56548-142-8

Trilogy on Faith and Happiness
paper, 978-1-56548-359-0

E-books Available

Essential Sermons, Homilies on the First Letter of John, Revisions, The Confessions, Trilogy on Faith and Happiness, The Trinity, The Augustine Catechism: The Enchiridion on Faith, Hope and Love.

Custom Syllabus

Universities that wish to create a resource that matches their specific needs using selections from any of the above titles should contact New City Press.

Free Index

A free PDF containing all of the **Indexes** from *The Works of Saint Augustine, A Translation for the 21st Century* published by NCP is available for download at www.newcitypress.com.

New City Press — The Works of Saint Augustine Catalog

For a complete interactive catalog of *The Works of Saint Augustine, A Translation for the 21st Century* go to New City Press website at: www.newcitypress.com

Electronic Editions

InteLex Corporation's Past Masters series encompasses the largest collection of full-text electronic editions in philosophy in the world. The Past Masters series, which include *The Works of Saint Augustine, A Translation for the 21st Century,* published by New City Press, supports scholarly research around the world and is now being utilized at numerous research libraries and academic institutions. The Works of Saint Augustine (Fourth release), full-text electronic edition, is available for subscription from InteLex. The Fourth release includes all 41 of the published volumes as of May 2016. For more information visit: http://www.nlx.com/home.

 About the Augustinian Heritage Institute

In 1990, the Augustinian Heritage Institute was founded by John E. Rotelle OSA to oversee the English translation of *The Works of Saint Augustine, A Translation for the 21st Century.* This project was started in conjunction with New City Press. At that time, English was the only major Western language into which the Works of Saint Augustine in their entirety had not yet been attempted. Existing translations were often archaic or faulty and the scholarship was outdated. These new translations offer detailed introductions, extensive critical notes, both a general index and scriptural index for each work as well as the best translations in the world.

The Works of Saint Augustine, A Translation for the 21st Century in its complete form will be published in 49 volumes. To date, 42 volumes have been published.

NEW CITY PRESS

About New City Press of the Focolare

New City Press is one of more than 20 publishing houses sponsored by the Focolare, a movement founded by Chiara Lubich to help bring about the realization of Jesus' prayer: "That all may be one" (John 17:21). In view of this goal, New City Press publishes books and resources that enrich the lives of people and help all to strive toward the unity of the entire human family. We are a member of the Association of Catholic Publishers.

Free Index to *The Works of Saint Augustine*

Download a PDF file that provides the ability to search all of the available indexes from each volume published by New City Press.

Visit http://www.newcitypress.com/index-to-the-works-of-saint-augustine-a-translation-for-the-21st-century.html for more details.